Moontouched
Moonstruck Book 2
USA Today Bestselling Author
Heather Young-Nichols

heatheryoungnichols.com

Also by Heather Young-Nichols

Rules of the Game

Kissing the Player

Wanting the Player

Moonstruck

Moonstruck

Moontouched

The Empowered Series

The Gremlin Prince

The Goblin War

The Gorgon Sacrifice

Shadow Coven

Haunted Magic

Cursed Magic

Stolen Magic

Fated Magic

Forever 18

Forever Grayson

Forever London

Forever Lennox

Heavy Hitter

Pushing Daisies

Daisy

Van

Bonham

Daltrey

Mack

Courting Chaos

Cross

Ransom

Booker

Dixon

Finding Love

Making Her Mine

With J.A. Hardt

Bound by Magic

With Amelia J. Matthews

Dirt on the Diamond

After Office Hours: Seducing the Professor

Chapter One

WAS this the calm before the storm? I thought so.

Since meeting Orin, there had been very few moments of calm. Right now, we were in one. Sort of. I didn't think my mind would know a moment's peace again. It hadn't been long, a month, since Orin's brother had died saving me, yet I couldn't get the image of him on the ground, bloody and dying, out of my head.

I wasn't asleep. This wasn't a dream. I would've been lucky if I'd been dreaming. A nightmare, I could handle. A nightmare, I could wake from. But this... this was a memory that was still haunting me when it didn't seem to be haunting anyone else.

Phillip... his name echoed in my mind. *Phillip, tell me what to do.*

Orin's fingers trailed up my bare leg before his hand squeezed my hip.

I was lying naked in bed with my shifter husband in a room that he'd created for us. Well, he'd moved in here before we'd met, but in the short time we'd been together, he'd made sure it felt like home to me.

I was such a different person from the girl he'd met at my father's ball. That had been months ago. I'd been but a girl, and now... I didn't know what I was. When he'd walked into my life at the start of the season of 1923, I'd been meant to marry someone else. A man my father had chosen.

Since that day, I'd met Orin, run off to marry him when I'd barely known him, discovered that werewolves were real, he was one as was my mother, and watched as he'd fought off another pack of wolves who'd wanted me for breeding purposes.

My stomach clenched at the thought of it. Breeding. My own mother had died in childbirth. Her pack, the Balodis, had their numbers dwindling due to the mothers dying in childbirth. That was why they needed me, or any other part wolf-type creature to continue their line.

At this point, I didn't know what I was.

Allegedly, I was part wolf shifter, but I'd never

seen any sign of that. It was what had led Orin to me. His mate. Chosen by the fates, hated by his family.

"I can hear your mind racing from here," Orin whispered into my ear.

The morning sun was brightly streaming through the thin curtains that still hung over the windows. Living in a more southern climate meant we'd cool off the further into fall we went but weren't likely to get cold and rarely saw snow.

"What are you thinking about?" he asked quietly.

How could I tell him his brother haunted me? I didn't want to, but I also couldn't lie to him. Not after everything he'd done to protect me.

"Phillip." I bit into my bottom lip to keep the tears from falling. Tears were useless at this point.

Orin ran a hand across my stomach before pulling me back to his chest. "I explained that." It was a matter of fact, but there was pain behind his words.

"I know. I know you did." Then I turned so that I could face the man I loved. The only man who'd ever loved me. "That doesn't mean I don't still feel guilty. If you'd never have found me, your brother would still be alive."

Orin swallowed hard and pushed his fingers into

my hair, gripping the back of my neck so that he could bring my forehead to his lips. After kissing me there, he pressed my forehead to his.

"And I'd only be half alive," he whispered against my lips. "I'd give anything to have my brother back. For Diana to have her mate and Ruby to have her father. Anything but give up you." He squeezed the back of my neck.

"I know, but..." There was no use starting an argument with Orin. I'd never convince him that they all would've been better off if they'd left me with the Balodis pack. Knowing what they would've done to me... He'd never say his brother's death wasn't worth it.

No matter how sad it made him.

"My brother sacrificed himself for me, as I would do for any of them," he explained, still holding me to him. When I furrowed my brows, he took it as confusion, but really, I didn't like to hear that he would've had no problem being killed. The reason didn't matter. Including saving me. "My brother saved you for me. I would save any of their wives for them. It's the way this works. Losing a brother is hard, I'll not deny that. But losing your mate..." He shook his head.

I pushed up on my elbow so that I was over him, my hair fell over my shoulder. "Then Diana—"

He shook his head. "My parents are taking care of her. She'll be all right with time. Ruby will also be well cared for. You don't have to worry about them."

I closed my eyes tightly and swallowed hard. "I can't forget the image of..." Phillip's body lying in front of me, bloody and ripped apart.

"I know." He brought his thumb up to trace over my cheekbone. Every single touch warmed me from the inside out and calmed the storm raging inside of me. I suspected that he knew this and that was why he touched me so much. The other men I knew didn't do this with their wives. At least not in public, but Orin had no issue touching me even if people were watching. "I wish you never would've seen that and I can't erase those images from your mind. All I can do is replace them." Instead of doing something that would take this whole day in a completely different direction, Orin paused, looking out the window at nothing, and then said, "But not now, I guess."

One of the doors downstairs opened and then shut loudly, as if whoever had entered wanted to make sure we knew they were there. Orin would've known someone had been coming long before I could hear them.

He sighed. "My brother." Then he kissed me quickly and jumped out of bed. After grabbing the pants he'd worn yesterday, which were still on the chair in the corner, he pulled them on, though I wondered why he didn't put his boxer shorts on first. "I'll go see what he wants."

I sat up, holding the sheet to my chest. "I'll get dressed and be right down."

He scanned the skin he could see then shrugged. "I'd honestly rather you didn't."

I had to laugh at how disappointed he sounded at the idea of me putting clothes on. Still, he left the room while pulling his shirt up his arms.

Once he was gone, I hurried out of bed and pulled an outfit out of my closet. Since being with Orin, I'd been able to rid myself of some of the stricter parts of society. He wanted me to be comfortable with whatever I wore. Including my hair. It'd always been long and pinned back. That was a strict rule.

Not anymore.

I'd recently had it cut and it now fell to just below my shoulders. My natural wave gave my hair movement and texture. I hadn't even known my hair had a wave until that day.

But since I wasn't leaving the house, I left my hair down and put on my underwear—sans required corset—before donning a pair of trousers with a shirt that buttoned up, then followed that with my everyday shoes that didn't have a tall heel.

I never knew how much more comfortable I could've been all of these years. My father had insisted on heels at all times and I was to never leave my room without being fully decent.

Surprisingly, it only took me ten minutes to get ready. In the old days, I'd needed at least an hour. There was a freedom that came from being with Orin. A freedom that brought whispers and looks when I was in town, but I didn't care. I was sure things were reported back to my father, but since Orin paid him, he had no say in my life whatsoever.

Maybe I'd even start a trend.

When I got down the stairs, I could just see into the kitchen, where Roman was sitting at the table with a cup of coffee in front of him. Orin was at the end of the table with a cup of his own.

"You two are ridiculous," Karina said from somewhere else in the room.

Roman was the middle child in their family. Number three out of five boys. Orin was the youngest. The two of them—actually all of the boys—looked alike. Dark hair and dark eyes that seemed to see into your very soul and they were all incredibly tall, as were their parents. When they were all in the same room, I felt like a child among the adults, given how much smaller I was. Some in his family thought I was frail, but I wasn't. I just wasn't a huge shifter.

Karina, Roman's wife, was also a shifter, though I'd never seen most of them shift. Only Orin and his father when his father had found out about me. But Karina wasn't all dark in her coloring. She did have darker blonde hair, but it was eons lighter than the hair of the Vilkatas men. Her eyes were hazel and twinkled in the sunlight. She was absolutely beautiful.

I walked slowly into the kitchen, still feeling a little shy around his family, given that they'd contributed so much to my safety and I could contribute nothing to theirs. Also, knowing that part of the reason Roman and his wife stayed while the rest of the family left had been to keep ensuring my safety. Orin hadn't let me go anywhere alone since the day they'd gotten me back.

"You don't have to be so timid," Karina said before she could see me.

I was still getting used to the fact that they could all probably hear my heartbeat or my muscles working inside my body with their shifter hearing. The day I'd found out that everyone in the house could hear Orin being intimate with me... was still embarrassing.

"I'm not," I told her as I fully entered the room. "I didn't want to interrupt."

"You couldn't," Orin told me, those dark eyes causing flames to lick across my skin.

"Want some breakfast?" Karina asked in my own kitchen. Of course, they all knew that I was still learning to cook.

"Maybe just some eggs. I can make them." I moved in that direction, but she turned around with a pan already full of scrambled eggs.

"Already done," she said with a smile. "These two were complaining about being hungry."

The Vilkatas family was much less formal than what I'd grown up with. It was taking time, but I was getting used to it and even reveling in the fact that I could be less formal with them.

"Thank you," I told her before helping her bring the eggs, bacon, and toast to the table.

Orin pushed the chair closest to him out so that I'd know to sit there. He liked to have me close even in moments like this.

After taking a small amount of eggs, Orin furrowed his brows, so I sighed and took one more spoonful. It was like he'd forgotten that I didn't have the shifter appetite or their ability to burn off what I ate. Then I passed it to him and around the table they went.

"What were they being ridiculous about?" I asked Karina once everyone was settled.

"Everything," she said, which brought a round of laughter from the men. "In this case, it was the amount of eggs I needed to make."

"They thought you needed more?" I asked. She nodded as I glanced over at each of their plates. There was still some left in the pan, but not much. "They might've been right."

She laughed and took a forkful of her own food into her mouth. Karina was like the men. But she was a shifter, so she had a shifter appetite. She was still tall and athletic, most would've said. She was shapely like a woman, but strong like a man.

If I was being truthful, I was a little jealous of her. I had been raised to be a woman who was taken care of instead of one who took care of people. I was supposed to marry rich so that I'd never have to do anything except pop out a kid or two whom a nanny could raise.

The joke was on my father. I *had* married rich—Orin had more money in this house than I'd ever seen in person and he'd given a bunch to my father. He said it didn't even cover the tip of the iceberg. He might've been wealthier than my own father. Orin also didn't expect me to do things, but he knew that I wanted to and was in the process of making sure that I could.

Hence, cooking lessons. It was slow-going, but I was learning.

"Any news?" Orin asked his brother. Both Karina and I were listening intently.

Roman sighed. "Ivan and Daniel are still angry."

"Aren't we all?" Karina asked, causing my stomach to tighten. Karina had been on my side from the beginning and the idea that she blamed me for Phillip's death made all the guilt I felt on my own rise up. "We didn't get enough of the Balodis pack. I know I still want blood." My shoulders slumped slightly. "Not yours, Elizabeth." She patted my hand, which was lying on the table. "Theirs."

That was something, at least.

"We are all still angry," Roman confirmed. "But

the anger of the people at this table is directed at the right place. The rest of our family's isn't, necessarily."

Which meant it was directed at me.

"If I could've..." I started, but Orin cut me off.

"There was nothing you could do," he assured me again. "They're shifters, and you're... well, not human, but you might as well be."

He was right. I'd been defenseless against them all, which meant now I was determined for Orin to at least teach me how to protect myself a little. Maybe a weapon was in order.

"Once the sting of Phillip has worn off, they'll come around," Roman promised. The thing was that I thought the family had already started coming around. They had seemed to not hate me when they left, but maybe the reality had set in and I couldn't blame them.

"We're going to Boston," Orin said suddenly, filling me with renewed excitement. It was something we'd recently decided and hadn't told anyone yet.

"Boston?" Roman asked with an eyebrow raised.

Orin nodded. "Lizzie found her mother's sister. Apparently, they had been estranged since before she was born. She wants to meet her and maybe get some answers."

Meet her? Yes. Get some answers? Absolutely. She was the only person who knew what had really happened with my mother and her family since it was my aunt's family, too.

Roman glanced to Karina. "I guess we're going to Boston."

"No." I furrowed my brows. "You two just moved here. You have to get settled. I don't want to uproot your lives again." Since they were here because of me.

"You're not," Karina assured me. "But if you two are going, we're going. It's a pack thing." Though that didn't make any sense.

"How can it be a pack thing?" I glanced from her to Orin then back.

Karina wet her bottom lip. "The pack protects each other. We can't let the two of you go off on your own because the Balodis pack is still out there. There's no way they gave up on the idea of you helping repopulate their pack. We have to protect the two of you."

Now I was looking forward to the trip less. If I could've gone alone, I would've, but Orin would've never let that happen.

I was doing something selfish—going to Boston for information about my mother that probably wouldn't make a difference to our lives—and putting them all in danger.

Again.

Even knowing me was putting them in danger, and one of their pack had already been killed.

I wouldn't be able to live with myself if something happened to any more of them.

Chapter Two

There was no stopping Karina and Roman from going to Boston with us. Honestly, I stopped trying, given the fact that it would mean Orin wouldn't be left fighting off an entire pack of wolf shifters on his own should the other pack attack.

Hopefully, they wouldn't. This was something I was doing for myself to get to know my mother better.

"Do you have everything?" Orin asked as he stood in the doorway of our bedroom.

"I think so." I glanced at the pile of luggage waiting for him. It was a large trunk along with a suitcase and a case for my necessities. "I tried not to overpack." Though one thing I'd learned during everything that had happened recently was that I had to be prepared for everything. So while I'd packed the appropriate clothes for most circumstances, I added in some trousers and more sensible shoes.

I didn't want to be caught running in the woods in heels again.

"You're fine," he told me before picking up all of the bags. Sometimes his strength still surprised me. "Are you ready?"

I nodded then followed him out of the room, down the stairs, and out of the house. Roman and Karina were waiting by Orin's automobile. We'd go to the train station together.

Orin took care of everything when we got there. All I had to do was wait for him. Karina stayed by my side.

"Are you nervous?" she asked. At first, I wasn't sure what she was talking about. Then I realized that it had to be the fact that I was meeting my mother's sister for the first time. I'd never had family other than my father, so this was a first in many ways.

"A little," I told her honestly. "I've never really had family before. Until Orin."

"And your father?"

I shook my head. "My father gave me the life he did because he was obligated to. How would it look if he left an innocent baby uncared for? No. He did it because he had to and maybe a little because he loved my mother. Assuming he loved her at all."

Karina's eyes widened. "You don't think your father loved your mother?"

I shrugged. "I don't really know, but it's almost impossible to imagine that man loving anyone."

"You two look intense," Roman said when he came to a stop beside his wife. He looked at her, Adam's apple bobbing.

"Not intense," Karina said. "Well, not exactly. Elizabeth was telling me about her father." Her gaze jumped to Orin's. He was standing beside me and I felt all of his muscles tighten at the mention of that man. "Just a little. I asked if she was nervous to meet her aunt."

My husband grunted, but I could feel his gaze on me. He was probably more worried about me than he let on.

"Let's get on the train." He led the way.

Orin had gotten us a sleeper car while Roman and Karina went to the one next to it. They were like tiny hotel rooms on the train. It would be cramped, but I couldn't think of anyone I'd want to be cramped with other than Orin.

"What's this?" I asked while pointing at the thing folded up against the wall.

"It's a bed," he told me. "These are so small that they put two in."

When I looked around the small room, I realized it made sense to stack the beds that way. "Will you be sleeping up there?"

"We won't be using it."

A shiver ran through me. He intended to make the small, one-person bed work for us and I was looking forward to it.

The idea of being in bed with Orin used to make me blush. I almost couldn't have imagined the amount of pleasure that could come from sex with him, let alone how comfortable it would be to sleep with his arms wrapped around me.

"It's going to take two days to get to Boston, so I thought this would be much more comfortable."

It definitely would be.

We spent time with Roman and Karina in the dining car, but soon after, Orin wanted us alone in our car. As anxious as I was to get to Boston, the time flew by.

The moment we stepped off the train in Boston, we were surrounded by people. People who didn't seem to care we were there, as they had their own business to attend to, but it was more people than I'd ever seen in a single place.

Once again, Orin and Roman took care of everything, including finding a taxi cab to take us to our hotel. Who knew such things existed. We'd gotten in and the hotel was very accommodating. We were checked in, our bags were unpacked by the bellman, and now it was time to do what I'd come to do. I couldn't wait another minute. It was already afternoon.

Roman and Karina were going to come with us, but not into my aunt's house.

Orin gave another taxi cab driver the address to where we were going and once we were standing in front of the modestly grand house, my stomach was in knots. This woman had known my mother better than anyone else. She'd know things that I'd never find out otherwise and I couldn't believe my luck in finding her.

"You two stay in the area," Orin directed his brother. "You'll hear if we need help."

Karina squeezed my hand before the two of them walked away.

"Are you ready?" he asked quietly.

"Probably as ready as I'll ever be," I told him.

He took my hand and led me up to the house. After one last look, Orin knocked on the door.

When the door opened, the woman on the other side was a bit taller than me, but she had the same blonde hair and blue eyes that I did. She had to be my aunt. There were too many similarities.

"Audrey?" I asked with a lot of hesitation.

The corners of her mouth fell, then she said, "Elizabeth."

I almost let out a sob right there on her front porch. This was my mother's sister. She reached out and took my hand in hers, squeezing tightly.

"Come in," she finally said.

Audrey's house wasn't as large as my father's. He would've called it "working class," but it felt like a home, something I hadn't experienced until I'd moved into Orin's house. Audrey led us into the parlor.

"Please, have a seat. May I offer you refreshments? Tea? Coffee?" She glanced from me then to Orin.

"I would love some coffee," Orin told her, but I couldn't have taken anything in right then if I'd wanted to.

The woman standing before me was family. Familiar yet still a stranger.

"I'll be right back." Audrey left the room for several minutes before coming back. "It will be ready shortly." She took a deep breath then looked at me. "Elizabeth, I'm quite surprised to see you here."

"You knew who I was when you answered the door," I told her. There had to have been a reason for that.

Audrey smiled softly. "You look just like your mother. I'd know you anywhere."

Tears formed in my eyes that I tried to swallow back. Crying right now would be useless.

"I wish you would have written," Audrey said suddenly, making my eyebrows pinch together in confusion. Why wouldn't she want to *see* me? "It's dangerous for us to see each other."

"Dangerous?" Orin asked, sliding to the edge of his seat. "Why dangerous?"

Audrey swallowed hard but didn't answer him.

"Why would this be dangerous?" I asked. "Does it have to do with my mother?"

"I'm sorry." Audrey suddenly stood. "I'm going to have to see you out."

Why would she offer us coffee to push us out? It didn't make sense...

It took me a few seconds and Orin's insistence to stand, but I did it and followed my aunt to the front door. Orin went through first, but Audrey stopped me before I could.

"I so hope that you are happy, Elizabeth." Then she pulled me into her arms, holding tightly. "I'd love it if you continued to write me," she said as she let me go.

As soon as I'd stepped out of her house, she closed the door behind us and I heard the lock engage.

But I stood there, absolutely dumbfounded. Why would my mother's sister not want to see me in person? Why was it dangerous for us to be together?

Now, more than ever before, I wished that I hadn't given my father the journal back. Maybe they would've had the answers to those questions. Now, I was just left hanging.

"That wasn't the reunion I thought it'd be," I told my husband when we got to the sidewalk. Roman and Karina were rushing up to us.

"That was quick," Roman said, but he was looking at Orin. The brothers had the ability to have a conversation without saying a word. Sometimes, I wished that I could read their minds.

"Let's get dinner," Orin said instead of telling him what my aunt had said.

Another taxi cab ride later, we were in a restaurant that was not quite full. There were round tables in the dining area with white cloths. It was a nice place without being fancy. I wasn't dressed for any kind of dinner out, but we were here, anyway. Luckily, it didn't look like it was the kind of place that required formal dressing.

Once we were seated and ordered, Karina asked, "So what happened? Why weren't you in there long?"

Before Orin had a chance to respond, I said, "She offered coffee then told us it was dangerous for me to be there."

"Dangerous. Why would it be dangerous?"

I shrugged. "I don't know. I want to go back tomorrow." One look at Orin and I knew that he'd do whatever I wanted. If I wanted to chance rejection again tomorrow, he'd be there by my side.

"That doesn't make sense," Karina said. "Unless..." She dropped her voice. "Do you think she sensed us outside?"

"Sensed?" I asked, whispering like she was.

"If she's a shifter, she'd be able to sense us, right?"

"She should be able to," Orin told her. "I don't know if that was it or not. I guess we'll find out tomorrow."

Karina changed the subject after that and I was grateful. It was nice to enjoy dinner without worrying about the oddity of what had happened at my aunt's house. My mind was already consumed with the possibilities of what she might be afraid of. I didn't need it to take over the conversation as well.

At least we got to eat in peace. We all ordered the ham and potatoes and though I barely tasted it going down, what I did taste was delicious.

After Orin paid, the four of us left the restaurant.

The weather was still nice enough that I didn't need to wear a coat just yet. I had one back at the hotel should the need arise. But for now, walking with my arm wrapped around my husband's was good enough. As Orin and I turned the corner, a man bumped into my shoulder. I was about to excuse myself when I was hit with...

The man hurried out into the road. An auto honked its horn and then something screeched before the worst sound I'd ever heard echoed in the air. The man's body flew and landed with a wet thud on the concrete.

I gasped.

"What is it, Elizabeth?" Orin asked, his eyebrows drawing together as he tilted his head, keeping his eyes strongly on me.

"Did you just see...?"

When I looked, the man was still standing on the sidewalk not far from us.

But I'd just seen him hit by a car. How could he be standing on the sidewalk?

"Did we see what, Elizabeth?" This time, it was Roman, leaning in as he came even closer to me.

"I just saw that man..." If I told them that I saw a man who was standing on the sidewalk perfectly fine get hit by a car, they'd have me committed to an asylum. I surely didn't want that.

Then the man hurried out into the road. An auto honked its horn and something screeched. There was a thump and the man's body flew back, landing with a wet thud against the concrete.

Just as I'd already seen happen.

It was an intense feeling of déjà vu. That I'd been here and done this before. Because I just had.

Roman and Orin ran out to the street, as did many other men, but I slowly began to step back until I hit the side of the building closest to us.

"Elizabeth?" Karina asked. "Are you all right?"

My body was vibrating and I couldn't form words. "I... I..."

She stepped closer to me. "What happened, Elizabeth?"

"I saw that man get hit."

"We all did. Roman and Orin are trying to help him."

"No." My gaze finally found hers, focusing in on her dark eyes. "I saw it before it happened."

Her brows pinched together. "What?"

Before I could explain further, our men were back. I was still shaking with my body pressing against the building when Karina asked if the man was all right.

"He's dead," Roman told her. "We need to get out of here."

Without explaining why, Orin had me tucked under his arm and began walking as quickly as my legs would carry me until we were inside the hotel lobby.

"We'll see you two in the morning," he said as he kept us moving, though a little more slowly, to the lift, which took us to the floor we were staying on.

Inside the room, Orin locked the door behind us then turned to me.

"Are you all right, Lizzie?"

I was honestly getting tired of people asking me that question, but no. I wasn't all right. Not at all.

But how could I explain what had happened to him without him thinking I'd lost my mind?

"I…"

"It's a lot. I know." He wrapped his arms around me tightly. He meant seeing the man die, but it was seeing him die twice that really had me off-balance.

How could I have seen it twice? I hadn't. That was the only explanation I could come up with.

Except I had. Now I needed to ground myself back in reality before I thought I'd lost my mind.

"Make me feel better," I said, but I didn't recognize my own voice. "Make me feel better, Orin."

"Anything, Lizzie," he whispered against the top of my head.

I stepped back just enough to reach my hands up and cup both of his cheeks so that I could bring his mouth down to mine.

At first, Orin didn't respond and then he did.

This was the only thing I knew how to do that might make me feel better and convince myself that I hadn't seen that man die in my mind before he died on the street.

Chapter Three

"I'll make you feel more than better," Orin said once he'd brought that kiss to an end. I knew he could. That was why I was turning to him now.

Seeing what had happened to that man on the street—twice—was more than I could take. If only I'd have gotten the words out of my mouth quicker, maybe he'd still be alive. The scene that had played out in my head before it'd played out in front of my eyes had left me breathless, tilted, too horrified to speak.

Orin could make it better.

"You want me to touch you?" he whispered, sending tiny prickles of pleasure out over my skin before he'd really touched me.

I swallowed hard, not able to tell him exactly

what I wanted. We'd come a long way since the first time we'd been intimate, but I wasn't to the place where I could just ask for what I wanted. Technically, I already had. I'd told him I needed him to make me feel better.

My eyes fluttered closed as I took a deep breath.

I could do this. Orin was my husband and there was nothing wrong with wanting him the way I did every second of my life.

Slowly, I moved up onto my tiptoes and pressed my lips to his. A low growl never made it out of his chest. This was new. There were pitiful few times that I made the first move to be with Orin, yet every time that I did, it affected him in a way that I couldn't describe.

His tongue swept over my lips, threatening to make me lose every ounce of control I had. The control that would've made me an obedient wife to someone else. That was the person I was supposed to be, not the person I was now.

Orin's kisses were brutal as he pushed his hands into my hair and held tightly, tipping my head to his preferred angle. There was no doubt that he was now fully in control. Hip lips were soft, his tongue like silk. Alone, they were almost able to make me forget what I'd seen in the street.

No. I needed more.

I curled my hands tightly against the fabric of his shirt, pulling him closer as his tongue explored every inch of my mouth. Every pass, every movement, made me greedy, needy, suddenly so hot that I needed my clothes off. He'd take care of that soon enough. With his one hand in my hair, his other arm wrapped around my waist and lifted me off the ground. Orin held me with such ease—as if I weighed nothing at all. But I did weigh something.

Orin was just strong.

His mouth left mine, then his lips trailed over my jaw then down my neck, tasting me, scraping his teeth against my sensitive skin.

"Orin." My voice was strangled and didn't sound like me at all. I pulled at his shirt again, which made him move away from me just enough to rip the buttons apart. The sound of the small circles scattering over the floor meant that I'd likely never find them all.

I didn't even care. All I wanted was to be able to touch him. To remind myself that he was there, he was mine, and he'd protect me.

Orin was much gentler with my shirt. His buttons were easy to put back on. My clothes were more delicate. He slid his hands under my top, the first touch of his skin against mine burning me in the most delicious way. He ran hotter than me on a normal day, but this... was something else. Something more.

"Elizabeth," he whispered against my skin. "I need you naked."

And I needed him naked.

Orin pushed my shirt up over my head then scraped his nails over the fabric of my brassiere. This was a time when most of the women my age wore bandeau versions to flatten their breasts. I, however, took some of the new fashions and put it with the old. Given the curves of my body, I was never going to achieve the androgynous, flat look that the flappers went for. So I wasn't going to try.

With almost no effort, my brassiere was gone and my nipples hardened in the cool air. Orin groaned again when he stepped back to look. Then he took one in his mouth. I curled my fingers into his hair, enjoying the desire coursing through me and the feel of his mouth on me.

He'd put that mouth in places that I hadn't known men used their mouths. When I'd come to him, I'd been sheltered, innocent.

I was much less so now.

As he let the nipple pop from his mouth and

moved to take the other in, he pulled my skirt down my legs, followed by my panties and garter belt. He kissed down my stomach as he pushed my stockings down, leaving me completely naked in front of him.

He sat back and slowly trailed his eyes down me, something that felt as real as his touch, until he was looking at the point where my legs met my body.

My cheeks burned. Not so much from embarrassment—he was my husband, this was normal—but from what I knew was coming next.

"There are a lot of ways that I love you, Elizabeth Vilkatas." He sighed. "But this might be the one I love the most."

It might've been the wrong timing, but I snickered.

Orin's big hands grabbed my thighs and began moving me back until I fell onto my bottom on the bed. Then he pushed my thighs apart as far as they would go. Before I could lie back, his head was between my legs and he licked me.

Once again, I curled my fingers into his hair. Orin knew exactly what he was doing when he gently pushed the spot between my breasts so that I would lie back. With my hand still in his hair, he pulled me closer to the edge and pushed my knees apart even more.

This left me open to whatever he wanted to do, but I wanted it all. There wasn't anything he could've done that I would have said *no* to.

"You taste so fucking good," he said, the harsh, dirty words making my entire body blush. That was probably what he wanted. He loved it when my skin flushed.

The thing about Orin—and his family—was that they weren't like the society I'd grown up in. They weren't as formal. They didn't have the rules. They were more modern than the flappers, who were known for sex before marriage with more than one man if they wanted.

They did what they wanted when they wanted and with who.

It was a freedom that I'd craved. A freedom I'd found with Orin.

His tongue was replaced by his wet fingers, circling around my center. In my father's world, just knowing that was the clitoris—as Orin had called it— was the sign of a deviant whore of a woman. According to Orin, it was my body. I should know what everything did.

I'd even said I'd ask Karina once, but Orin had insisted that he'd be the one to teach me anything I wanted to know.

It had been an education, for sure.

Soon, those fingers left my center and then pushed inside me. I dropped my head back with a groan. Everything Orin did brought the next level of pleasure, though I never asked him how he was so good at all of this.

That was something not so different from our cultures. Men had experience. It was to be expected.

As his fingers worked their way inside me, Orin licked my clitoris again. That was all it took. My orgasm slammed into me with the force I imagined would come from hitting a concrete wall. Wave after wave rushed over me, and I was unable to keep my sounds quiet.

Worse than the fact that people in the hotel might've heard me... his brother and sister-in-law could hear me no matter what. Their wolf hearing was very sensitive.

Once the waves subsided, Orin was over me, kissing me as he pushed inside me.

"Damn, you're tight today." His voice wavered, as if he were holding back.

I wasn't tight. He was big. We were getting close to the full moon and everything about him got bigger the closer to the full moon we got. I relaxed, knowing it was going to take more than one attempt for him to get all the way inside me.

Today, it took three.

Once he knew I'd grown accustomed to him, he was no longer holding back. Orin was always on the verge of being able to hurt me and this vulnerable time wasn't any different. If he let his animal loose when we were this close to the full moon... I'd probably never walk again.

Instead, it was a controlled ravaging.

Orin and I had sex many different ways. Sometimes, it was a slow coming together when we had all the time in the world. Sometimes, it was what he called a "quick fuck" against a wall, like what had happened the first time I'd touched him after he'd shifted. He'd said he'd never had such an overwhelming need to be inside me until that day.

Sure, he'd wanted me, yearned for me, done things that women like me weren't supposed to know about because of me. But that day, it had been a primal need that could've only been satisfied one way. And he'd never felt it with anyone else.

Probably because I was his mate, which meant there was a bond that couldn't be broken. Even if we were never able to be together, he told me that he'd never be far so that he could protect me.

Orin's skin warmed with tiny beads of sweat dotting his forehead as he pushed for his own release. Three more pumps and he found it.

He collapsed against me, caging me in with his huge body. But then he pushed his weight to one arm before lifting off me.

Tomorrow, there would be muscles hurting that I didn't even know I had. That much, I could be sure of.

When I lifted myself off the bed to head to the bathroom so that I could clean up the mess he'd just made, I stopped in front of him and lifted onto my toes so that I could kiss his jaw. As I walked away, he gave my bottom a slap.

Everything we'd just done should've embarrassed me. Yet with Orin, it never did. I quickly washed myself off before looking in the mirror to find my skin marked with tiny, red spots—the places that Orin had scraped his teeth a little too hard. At least they'd be gone in the morning. He was always sure to never draw blood and never go so deep that the evidence would be there for someone to find the next day.

Soon enough, I had put my nightgown on and was snuggled up in bed with my husband. He waited until I was pressed into his side with my head on his shoulder before wrapping his arm around me. Then he kissed the top of my head while I drew circles on his hard abdomen.

"Did it work?" he asked quietly. "It sounded like it worked."

I smiled against his chest, glad that I wouldn't have to look at him when I answered. "It worked, all right. Exactly how I wanted it to." Then I yawned and stretched all the way to my toes.

Yup. Sore muscles tomorrow, for sure.

"Good." He kissed the top of my head then leaned over to turn the light off.

At least sleeping wrapped up in Orin meant that I probably wouldn't have any nightmares.

The next morning, Orin, Roman, Karina, and I were in the restaurant of the hotel getting breakfast.

Today, I'd chosen to wear trousers with a silk, white shirt tucked into the belt. Orin had managed to get me a pair of men's wingtips small enough to fit me.

Hey. If the decade wanted androgyny, there was more than one way to achieve it. I'd gotten looks when we'd come to sit, but Karina was dressed simi- larly and didn't seem to notice the attention her clothing drew, so I wouldn't care, either.

"What are we doing today?" Roman asked before

taking a piece of steak in his mouth. He'd ordered steak and eggs while I'd asked for ham and eggs. There was no way I'd be able to eat a whole steak in the morning.

"I'd like to go back to my aunt's house," I told him, glancing at Orin with the hope that he wouldn't argue.

"I figured as much," he said. "We came all this way. We can't give up after one try."

"That's what I was thinking," I told him. "I'd like to get through to her. She's the only one who can tell me about my mother and maybe she'll have some information about why the Balodis are focused on me."

Orin's jaw clenched. "We know why."

"Yes." I put my hand on him to keep him calm. "But she might have more information. Or know how we can put an end to the Balodis coming for you for good." I sighed. "I don't know, but I'd like to try again."

"She'll probably be expecting you," Roman offered. "Can she shift? She might do it just to be alerted to us sooner."

"I don't know. She really didn't tell me anything."

I focused on my food while Orin and Roman

made a plan for going to my aunt's house. With everything that had happened, we couldn't just show up. They would need to have a serious plan with backups for what to do if things went wrong. I'd leave that to them while I tried to figure out what I could say to my aunt to get her to talk to me.

Soon, we were back at my aunt's house. Roman and Karina were going to the same park as they had yesterday when we'd been here. They'd be on alert, look for any approaching dangers, and come if Orin needed them.

I knocked on the door.

A large man answered, looming over me as if I were a danger. Orin cleared his throat so the man would know there wasn't anything he could do about me standing on the front porch.

"Is Audrey in?" I asked, my voice betraying me when it wavered. This man might not have intimidated Orin, but he sure intimidated me.

"She's not seeing anyone right now." He stepped back like he was going to close the door.

"I just need to—"

"What did I say?" he snapped as he stepped out in front of me.

"Watch it." Orin growled.

"Or what?" he spat. "Are you going to turn right here on the front porch?"

"You know?"

"Of course I know. I'm Audrey's husband. She wouldn't keep anything from me. But as I said, she's not seeing anyone. You're wasting your time."

"It's my time to waste."

"It's my wife's time you'd be wasting. Now go away." The man went back into the house, but before he could shut the door, I sprang into action.

Using a courage that I didn't think I had, I was in the house, ducking under his arm to find my aunt.

"Hey." Her husband reached out and grabbed my hand. Then I heard skin slap against skin.

Through clenched teeth, Orin demanded, "Drop her arm."

My apparent uncle dropped my arm but turned back to Orin, each of them ready to fight for the woman they loved. Except in our case, I was Orin's mate. He'd *die* before he let something happen to me.

I hurried to the room where my aunt had taken us when we'd first been here and she sat in the exact same spot as then as well.

"Please, Audrey. Please." I begged her and I wasn't proud of it, but I needed to hear what she had to say. "My father was awful. Life without my mother was awful. He promised me to men who would've hurt me because it helped his business and got rid of me." I took a quick breath as her mouth dropped open in evident surprise. "I need to know my mother."

"Your father wasn't nice to you?" she finally asked.

"No. No, he wasn't. I'll tell you anything that you want to know, just... Please."

Audrey looked me in the eye like she was trying to see into my soul, then she nodded.

"Edward," she said softly. The man who had answered the door came closer to her, leaving Orin right behind me. "We're going to need some tea," she told him.

"Are you sure?" he asked and she nodded.

He left the room before she said, "Tea for real this time. No playing tricks on you, I promise. We'll talk about your mom, but first... I need to know what you know." She glanced at Orin then back to me.

"I'll tell you everything," I told her. "Anything."

"Why did you chase us off before?" Orin asked as if I hadn't just offered every detail of my life up to the aunt that I'd just met.

Audrey winced then nodded. "I realized that my

husband was due home." Though the way she wouldn't meet my eye gave me the impression that it wasn't the full story. "I needed to talk to him before he found you here."

Orin considered her for a long moment then looked over to me. He didn't think it was the full story either but we were going to accept this explanation and not push her. I needed answers and couldn't risk getting on her bad side before I got them.

She sighed. "I hope you're ready for a long day."

If it meant knowing more about my mother, I'd stay there as long as it took.

Chapter Four

Audrey moved to the sofa right behind her and sat down slowly. She moved so purposefully, so gracefully... It wasn't all that dissimilar from how Orin sometimes moved.

Sometimes, he moved like a bull, and other times he glided like a swan. Maybe no one else noticed it, but I did.

"Please," she said, patting the other side of the cushion next to her. "Sit."

With hesitation, I glanced back at Orin and then at her. This was my mother's sister, yes. But I also didn't know her and given everything that had happened with the Balodis pack, I'd become quite wary of people I didn't know. If Orin was with me, I

knew I'd be fine. But this would put me in close prox-
imity to her.

Still, if I wanted to know everything about my
mother, where she'd come from, why the pack was so
focused on me, I'd have to trust her a little.

So I took a step forward. Before I could get very
far, Orin's large hand wrapped around my arm to
stop me.

"She'll be safe with me," Audrey told him as
Orin glared at her with a tight jaw. He was already
on alert, which of course, he would be.

"Orin," I said quietly as I turned to him. He loosened his grip on my arm but didn't let go. "I'll be all
right," I told him, then I lowered my voice further.
"You'll know if I'm not, right?"

A low growl percolated in his chest.

Audrey sighed before adding, "You'll be able to
hear everything from the kitchen, won't you?" Orin's
gaze swung from me to her. "Edward will make you
coffee. I prefer tea, but I have a hunch that you'll
want the coffee."

Finally, Orin released my arm and leaned in so
that only I would hear. "I'll be very close."

Behind me, Audrey chuckled, which meant she'd
heard him. Of course she had. She would have been
a wolf shifter like my mother. Or at least, that was

our impression of the Balodis pack. Since the Balodis were my mother's people, they were Audrey's people.

"Edward," she said again without raising her voice. That had to mean that either her husband was also a shifter with their accentuated hearing or he was close by enough that she didn't have to shout.

Edward appeared, carrying a tray with a teapot and two cups. He sat that on the table then turned back to Orin and pointed in the direction he'd just come. Orin hesitated until Audrey made a brushing movement with her hands.

"You'll hear if she's not all right."

That seemed to do the trick because he was still reluctant, but he followed her husband anyway.

"Men," she said with a sigh. "They never trust that we women can take care of ourselves."

I took small steps to get to the sofa where she was and sat on the very end. As far from her as I could get just to give Orin an extra few precious seconds to get to me if things went wrong. Except my instinct told me she wasn't going to hurt me. My instinct also might've been garbage, but it was all I had.

"Elizabeth, darling." Audrey reached out to take my hand in hers, which forced me to scoot across the cushion of the sofa.

Audrey resembled what I imagined my mother would have looked like now. I had one picture of my mother. She was young and beautiful in it. The lightness of her in the photograph had me imagining that her hair had been blonde like mine. Audrey's was, even if it was starting to fade. My aunt also had the same blue eyes as I did, which left me hope that those had also been from my mother.

She hadn't been there for me growing up and I wanted to cherish any little thing that she might've given me. Even if it had been genetics and not on purpose.

"Oh, Elizabeth." Her voice almost sounded watery and when she swallowed hard, I knew she was fighting back tears. "I never dreamed you and I would ever meet. You look so much like my sister." The back of her hand gently caressed my cheek. "You could almost be her twin."

"You're her older sister, right?" That was something safe we'd covered in the letters we'd exchanged.

"Yes. Only by a year. Actually, we aren't... weren't even a full year apart."

"What was it like?" I asked, my own eyes filling with tears. For the first time in my life, I was talking openly with someone who'd known my mother. "Growing up with her? What was she like?"

"Well, what did your father tell you about her?" Her blue eyes searched mine for the truth that I wouldn't have been able to hide even if I'd wanted to.

"Nothing," I confessed. "Almost nothing. He told me that she died in childbirth, but the topic was, like anything else, completely off limits."

Her brows furrowed. "He didn't tell you how they met? About their wedding? About how much she wanted you?"

I shook my head, my blonde curls bouncing at my shoulders. "He didn't even tell me that she had a sister."

"Well, that makes sense. He didn't know about me." Audrey poured each of us a cup of tea and though I didn't want any, I took it, anyway. It'd give me something to do with my hands.

"He... He didn't know." I stirred two cubes of sugar into my tea. That was how I would've drank it if I were going to.

"No." She cleared her throat then took a small sip from her cup. "She met him and... it was just better that he didn't know about me. Once she was set to marry him, I left and came to Boston. It was better for the two of us to split apart." She set the cup and saucer onto the table. "What do you know about our family? You mentioned knowing something."

It'd been one letter. Then I'd received one from her and had become set on coming here. But I had mentioned the Balodis pack.

I took a deep, calming breath. The memories I was about to churn up weren't going to be pleasant. "Yes. The Balodis took me about a month ago. They said that I belonged to them. Through that, we found out that they were my mother's pack." This was even harder than I thought and the churning in my stomach made me very glad I hadn't taken even a sip from the tea. "Your pack."

She closed her eyes briefly and nodded. "My father's pack."

"Not your mother's?"

Orin had explained to me that belonging to the same pack didn't automatically mean you were from the same bloodline. Families could join or leave packs, though both were incredibly hard to do and involved things he hadn't wanted to tell me about.

"Not my mother's," she echoed.

Now I had more questions. It'd been such a big deal that Orin had claimed me because I wasn't part of the pack—or rather, because I was human—that I had assumed you were destined to marry within your own. Apparently, that wasn't the case.

"Tell me about your husband," she said instead of elaborating.

Fighting a smile, I said, "He found me. Or rather he came to me. Orin said that his search for his mate had led him to me. But I was supposed to be a wolf shifter. At that time, I knew nothing about any of it. Then I was just human. Until the Balodis showed up and tried to also put a claim on me."

Phillip, tell me what to do, echoed in my head before I could shake off the memory.

"Orin lost a brother to get me away from them. I'm not entirely sure it was worth it."

A growl echoed from the kitchen, reminding me that Orin could hear every word that I said. He'd assured me time and again that he would've done the same to protect Phillip's wife. It was all part of being brothers. Still, the guilt threatened to eat me alive on a near-daily basis.

"I'm sure his brother thought it was." She leaned back to take the measure of me, searching what she could see for leftover signs of injury, I thought. "Did they violate you? The pack can be ruthless. They'll stop at nothing to find what they want."

"No." That was one thing they hadn't done. "One of them, Peter, made sure that no one touched me until it was decided who would…" I swallowed hard. "Get to have me."

Her eyes widened. "Peter is my brother. Adopted," she said pointedly, as if that would've made it any better if he'd been the one chosen to have me. "He was very young when we left." Which would've been at least twenty-one years ago, since that was my age.

But I realized I needed more information. "How long before I was born did you and my mom leave?"

The guard that had been in her eyes before I'd mentioned her brother slammed back into place. Almost as if she'd let it down briefly and regretted it.

"Not long," she told me. "Do you know anything about how your parents met?"

I shook my head and set the ever-cooling tea cup I'd been holding on the table. "He didn't like to talk about her."

Her eyes closed slowly again. "Probably too hard for him."

I didn't think that was it, but I wasn't about to correct her. I still wanted information from her.

"Can you please tell me about her family?" I practically begged. "*Your* family."

"I'd have to start with our parents." I would've been happy if she started with her third cousin's husband's best friend's dog. I had no information and anything she told me would be more than that. "Our parents married for love."

I pinched my brows together. "Was that unusual?"

She smiled softly, as if she were lost in her own memories. "It wasn't completely unusual, I was told, but not exactly usual. Parents had a lot of say in whom a wolf would marry. Within the pack of course was preferred, but in an ally pack was allowed. But usually, even if it was a love match, the family had a heavy hand in the decision."

A humorless laugh came from my chest. "I do know what that's like."

She bit her lips together in what looked like sympathy. "My mother was none of those things. She wasn't from our pack or an ally pack."

"Was she from an enemy pack?"

"No." Did that mean...

"Was she human?"

"No."

The tightness forming in my chest was my body's way of trying to prepare me for whatever was coming next. Not a shifter. Not a human. What else was there in the world that I didn't know about?

Audrey pushed up from the sofa and paced over

to the window, gazing out as if she were seeing a world that wasn't there. Maybe it was the one from her childhood.

"The Vilkatas pack is a prestigious one," she told me. "Everyone wanted to be their ally, fall under their protection. They were one of the strongest packs and weren't seeing... the things that a lot of the others were."

"What things?"

"Well, since my family took you for breeding purposes, I'm sure you already know." She moved back to sit in the chair nearest her end of the sofa. It was like she wasn't comfortable anywhere she was. "Women were dying too frequently. The bloodlines were getting diluted because some of the men were taking human wives. I'm told it was hell on Earth as far as the infighting went."

"So your mother..." I prodded, worrying that Audrey may cut us short again and I wanted as much as I could get before he demanded we leave.

"She saw my father's death," my aunt said. My eyes widened. Like I had with that stranger on the street. "She wasn't supposed to warn him, a decree by her father, but she had to. She couldn't fight it. Instead of ignoring it, she intervened and saved him. My father always said that he knew in that moment that they were meant to be. It wasn't even the mate call. He just knew."

"But since she wasn't a wolf, it was frowned upon?" I asked.

She snorted. "Very much so. It wasn't only because of what she wasn't, but because of what she was."

My heart thudded against my chest. No matter how hard I tried to get it to calm down, I knew that Orin could hear it and my nervousness would agitate him. "What was she?"

"A banshee."

Something crashed in the kitchen, sending me to my feet. If the other pack had found me, surely, Roman and Karina would've warned us.

Instead of an angry pack of wolves coming for me, only one very angry one stomped through the entryway. He was still in his human form, but his muscles were growing by the second.

"A banshee?" he raged.

"What's a banshee?" I asked, but they all acted like I wasn't even there.

"How could you keep that from her?" Orin yelled.

Audrey took a step forward, but otherwise acted

unbothered. "I didn't know her mother died. Her mother would've have told her."

"Orin," I snapped. "What is a banshee? What does that mean?"

"We're leaving," he demanded without answering me again. His hand wrapped around my arm and he began dragging me to the door, as if he weren't sure I was going to follow him.

"Orin." I pulled against his grip, but there was no budging him. "Tell me what's happening."

"I will. But not here."

"A banshee can see someone's upcoming death," Audrey said over the quiet anger of my husband that seemed to scream loudly in the room.

Orin's blood was rushing through his body with such a force that I would've sworn I could hear it.

"Like the man outside of the restaurant?" I asked, looking from one of them to the other.

It was then I realized that Edward had also come into the room and I didn't know how long he'd been there.

"Orin?" When he didn't answer, I turned back to my aunt. "Could my mother see people's deaths before they happened?"

"No." Her eyes were locked with Orin's as if they were having a silent conversation.

"Orin?" I pled.

Finally, his dark eyes found mine and softened. Then his grip on me softened as well. I bruised easily and he was always very aware of that. A loud crack of thunder burst over our heads as if the sky knew what was happening in this house.

"Don't leave just yet," my aunt said, but it wasn't to me. "I can explain. She needs to know. If you want to keep her safe, you need to know."

Everything about Orin changed, yet the anger still brewed beneath the surface. If I didn't know better, I'd say he needed to go for a run, but there wasn't any chance he was going to leave me, especially now.

I didn't know what a banshee was or what that meant for me, but his reaction told me it was a big deal.

Now I just needed to find out *how* big a deal it would be.

Chapter Five

"Please." Audrey was talking directly to Orin. "Come back in so we can discuss this."

I didn't know how she did it. Orin's anger was one of the scariest things I'd ever seen. Or it would've been if I hadn't been absolutely positive that he'd never do anything to hurt me. He had promised that the day I found him in the woods with the body of the man I had been betrothed to and had kept it. But that boiling rage hadn't fazed Audrey somehow.

"Orin," I whispered, knowing he'd hear it. This was important to me and I needed him to be OK with that.

"Fine," he said through clenched teeth. He agreed, but he wasn't happy about it.

"Come back in." She led the way back to the

room we'd just been in.

It was then that I realized that Orin had gotten me almost to the door. Reluctantly, he led the way to follow her. Edward also slipped into the room, but he remained standing near our only exit. I still didn't have a feel for that man, but Orin had spent some time with him and didn't appear to worry, so I wouldn't, either.

"What did you mean about the man at the restaurant?" she asked as soon as I sat on the sofa where she had been before. She put herself in the chair on that end so that Orin could be right beside me. Even she knew it was the only way he was going to let me stay.

"We saw a man hit by a car outside of the restaurant where we had dinner last night," Orin explained.

"No." The realization that I hadn't told even him what had really happened hit me like a wall. "Before that." I turned to face him. It was the only thing I could thing to do, given that I had lied by omission. "The man bumped into me and I saw... exactly what happened. But I saw it *before* it happened."

"A vision?" Audrey asked urgently, but I couldn't look at her. My eyes remained on my husband, whom I couldn't get a read on right now.

"Yes... or I think... I think so." I blew out a breath. "I don't know what happened. He bumped me and then I saw him step out into the street, get hit, and die. And then... I saw him step out into the street, get hit, and die. It was like... déjà vu, but all at once."

"You didn't tell me," he murmured, probably not wanting everyone to hear him.

"I know." Tears burned my eyes. "I didn't know what happened. I didn't know what I saw. I just... I just wanted to feel better."

And he'd done a fine job of making me feel better.

"That's not possible." It was like Audrey wasn't even talking to us anymore. Suddenly, her blue eyes snapped up to me. "Your grandmother disobeyed her family and the punishment was that the family put a hex on her. That hex says the banshee will remain dormant in her descendants. They wouldn't get the gift. That was to punish her and her descendants by extension since the way to break the curse is something we weren't willing to do."

"It's not a gift," I proactically yelled as a tear broke free and streamed down my face. "It's not a gift. I saw that man die—twice. There's nothing good about that."

Her brows furrowed and she lunged toward me,

forcing me back against the couch while Orin released a growl and the skin under my hand that was touching his arm began to change. He was going to shift. If he did that... he'd kill her.

"It is a gift," she said with a deadly calm voice that I almost didn't recognize. "It's a gift your mother or I would have done almost anything to have. If you can see a death coming, you can stop it. Keep those you love safe. There's no bigger gift than that."

"Step back." Orin growled, but it wasn't his voice. It was the one I'd heard before when he was part man, part animal. "Step back." That time, it was more animalistic.

My aunt knew what was good for her, so she moved away from me, giving me space to right myself. I scurried to my feet, not wanting to be taken off guard again.

"What's the thing you wouldn't do?" Orin asked, back to his human voice. The question wasn't for me. My aunt had said the way to break the curse was something neither she nor my mother would have done. That meant it had to be bad...

"What?" Again, he ignored me.

"What's the thing you wouldn't do to break the hex?" he demanded.

Audrey's chest rose and fell rapidly after the

interaction we'd just had. "Spill blood. We had to spill the blood of a family member. Neither your mother nor I wished to take a life. We wanted the gift to protect those we loved. To prevent those who would do more good alive from dying. We wanted to use it for good, but how could we do that if we had to commit such a heinous act?"

Orin's mouth snapped shut as he turned to look at me.

I'd done that. Or rather, I hadn't known I'd done that. I'd just been trying to break free of the Balodis pack and protect Karina. I hadn't even known the man, so there was no way I could've known he'd been a family member. I had just been trying to survive. Not trying to kill him.

I never would've done it if he hadn't been trying to kill the only person who'd acted like I wasn't a nuisance to their family at that time.

"It was with Karina in the woods," I mumbled. "I didn't know."

"Whether you knew or not, and honestly, I'd love to know who it was, it broke the hex. You probably don't touch a lot of people, so there would've been no way for you to know this would happen until outside of the restaurant."

Maybe Audrey was mad at me for killing the

man or for breaking the hex when she wouldn't benefit and that man would've been her family, even if distantly. I didn't know or care. All that mattered right now was getting the hell out of that house before I lost my mind.

My body vibrated as I looked up at Orin. "I have to go. I have to go now."

He nodded. "Then let's go."

He reached out to take my hand, but I snapped my back. "Please don't touch me," I whispered.

I didn't know if I was never going to touch my husband again if it meant I'd see his imminent death. That was something I couldn't handle and the fact that we'd been in danger—he'd been in danger because of me—pretty much the entire time we'd been together meant the chances of him dying were great.

I just didn't want to see it.

"Your grandmother could control it," Audrey said as we moved toward the door. "You could learn to control it as well. Only use it when you saw fit." We were through the door when she called out, "This doesn't have to be a curse."

The cool air hit my hot skin the moment I stepped out of the house. Before I got down the stairs, Roman and Karin were right there on the sidewalk.

"What happened?" Roman demanded. He was on alert without knowing why. It must've been a wolf thing.

"Not here," Orin said, standing too close to me. No matter how many times I tried to move away from him, he moved with me, which left him annoyingly close—too close for my comfort.

Karina was watching me as if trying to read my mind, my posture, the fact that I wouldn't allow Orin to touch me, but I wouldn't look her in the eye. If I did, she'd see the fear raging inside of me.

I wished there was a way to return the hex so I wouldn't have to worry.

She moved toward me. "Why don't we head back to the hotel?" But then she went to put her arm around my shoulders and I stumbled back several steps.

"Don't touch me," I said, louder than I should have, holding my hands up as if that would stop any of them. "None of you can touch me." My eyes burned with tears that I didn't want to fall. I was already becoming a monster. I didn't want to be the monster who cried all the time.

Then I turned and began walking toward the

hotel with my arms folded over my stomach and my eyes in front of me to make sure that no one touched me, even on accident.

"You can't touch her?" Roman whispered as if he thought I wouldn't hear him, but I didn't think the man had ever whispered in his life. "That'll be a fun marriage." Then he groaned like something hit him in the stomach.

"You two are being idiots," Karina told them quietly, though she didn't sound like she was trying to keep me from hearing. "What's going on, Orin?"

"We'll talk about it later."

It took a while to get back to our hotel. Of course, it didn't help that I took the wrong turn and ignored the Vilkatas behind me when they informed me of such. Nor did it help that I rejected all offers for a taxi. We'd have to sit too closely, which would've meant touching.

I didn't need Orin to direct me up to our room. That was where I was headed, anyway, given that I was holding on to my sanity by a very thin thread. I wanted to scream and cry and rail at the universe for making me this and taking away the one good thing I'd had in my life. My husband.

I needed time to think.

Orin and I had only been together for months,

but they'd been the best months of my life. Part of that included the time we'd spent in bed... or the sofa... or against the wall. Losing that now...

"Talk to me," he said quietly after shutting the door to our room. I'd say this for the Vilkatas family—they left me alone when I needed it. At least for a little while. "Tell me what's going on in that head of yours."

"Everything," I admitted. Just because I couldn't touch him didn't mean that I couldn't talk to him. "Everything is going on in my head and I don't understand most of it because it comes from your world."

"Not my world," he corrected. "My world isn't the banshee world."

"Why did that scare you? When she said the word banshee, you rushed out of the kitchen and I thought you were going to shift."

Orin took several steps, coming closer to me than I wanted him to. There wasn't anywhere for me to go, really. If I stepped back, I'd hit the wall. Then I'd be trapped. For now, I'd stay where I was as long as he didn't try to touch me.

"I wasn't scared," he said softly, then he swallowed hard. "I don't know much about banshees from experience. I've never met one."

"Until today," I added, once again trying not to cry.

Acting like I hadn't said anything, he continued. "I was worried. Not scared. What I do know of banshees isn't what I'd want for you."

"Tell me." I wrapped my arms under my breasts and steeled myself for whatever was to come. "Tell me what you know."

He sighed as he sat on the corner of the bed. "They have the power to see death. Obviously. But also the power to take a life with a single scream. I've heard that they have clairaudience—the power to hear things others can't."

"You have that."

He nodded. "The ability to identify names and objects." He shook his head quickly. "I could go on. I don't know if they have all those powers or only some of them. I just don't know." He dropped his hands onto his knees. "And I don't care. Right now, I want to know why you won't let me touch you."

Now, I couldn't stop the tears from falling. "Why?" I practically screeched. "Because I could see you die, Orin. I could see all of you die. I can't." The tears rushed down my cheeks like a waterfall on the side of a hill. My words caught in my throat and I let out a sob.

"Lizzie." He moved by—my vision was blurred, so I didn't know to where. It wasn't until his big hands wrapped around my upper arms that I knew he was right in front of me.

"No." I tried to pull away, but he wouldn't let me. The fight was slowly leaving my body, but I had to use every ounce of energy still inside me. I couldn't see him die right now and I would never know when I was about to have a vision. "Let me go, Orin." I choked on the words as they came out.

"No." His voice was calm and the words were spoken with finality. "Stop fighting me." I pulled two more times. "Elizabeth. Stop and listen to me for a moment."

That was when I decided to do as he said. I figured that if I let him say what he wanted, it'd be the quickest way to get him to let me go.

He leaned down so that he could look me in the eye. "There's no way that I can stop touching you. You're my mate. The one the universe wants me to be with. You heard your aunt. Your grandmother could control it. Which means you can to."

"I can't control it right now. I never know when I'll be hit with a vision of you dying."

"No." He loosened his grip. "It's going to take time and practice. We don't know how strong your powers are yet, given that you're only part banshee."

I furrowed my brows. "Part?"

"Your grandfather was a wolf. A Balodis. Your grandmother was a banshee. That means your mother was half of each. Then pair that with your father... It's only part. And we don't know what else is lurking in there."

"What do you mean... *lurking in there?*"

He stood back up and moved back toward the bed, taking me with him this time. When he lowered himself to the mattress, he was still almost my height.

"We don't know that all of your ancestors were full shifters. We'll have to talk to your aunt again, but, Elizabeth..." He gently ran his thumb over my cheek and jaw, tracing an invisible line down my neck. "I can't not touch my wife. My mate. You can't ask that of me."

As I quickly wet my lips, my breath quickened both from his touch and his words. Part of that was leftover worry from when I'd been promised to someone else. "Are you saying you'll touch me, anyway?"

His eyes widened and his jaw tensed. "No. I didn't fucking say that." He'd gotten loose with his tongue in the months we'd been together. "If you say *no*, I'll respect that, but it will kill me inside. I need you like I need to breathe."

Hesitantly, I pushed my fingers into his hair. "I don't know how to handle all of this right now. I could potentially watch you die over and over for the rest of our lives."

Orin lowered me into his lap so that my legs straddled his. This would've been impossible to do if I'd still worn a corset. Much to my father's dismay—probably—I was mixing the old styles with the new, but I hated girdles and Orin had convinced me that I didn't need to wear it.

His arms wrapped tightly around me. "Why not look at it as a gift, as Audrey said?" Before I could protest, he continued. "If you can see what's coming and that I'm in danger, we can stop it." His lips pressed gently against mine. "You could save me. Focus on that."

I'd been too scared at the prospect of seeing the man I loved die that I hadn't allowed that to sink in. Audrey said it could be used for good and while the fear was still there... I needed to push it aside. He had saved me. I could save him.

First, we'd have to determine exactly what I could do and I wasn't sure I was strong enough to find out.

Chapter Six

I HATED NOT TOUCHING ORIN. Hated it. But I kept my distance that night. Given that he was the one thing that comforted me in my times of need, losing that wasn't something I could stand, either. That put me in a bad spot.

Touch him and potentially watch him die over and over.

Not touch him and die inside little by little.

Honestly, there wasn't a choice.

Orin stayed as far from me in the bed as he could, his breathing telling me that he'd fallen asleep, but all I could do was stare at the ceiling. Having his warmth around me was what had let me sleep these past weeks since his brother's death. Somehow, the family was dealing with it far better than I was.

Or maybe they hid it better. I wasn't sure. Diana's scream when she'd seen him dead haunted me, much like Phillips's words. Neither was something I'd soon forget.

Giving in to my internal need and against my better judgment, I curled into Orin's side. As if he'd known I was going to do it all along, he wrapped a strong arm around me and pulled me even closer to him. Thankfully, no vision came.

"I knew you wouldn't last the night," he murmured with his cheek pressed against the top of my head.

"What can I say?" I asked. "I'm weak."

Orin used a single finger to raise my chin and bring my gaze to his. "Elizabeth, you're anything but weak. You're the strongest person I've met."

I furrowed my brows, but hearing the words made my eyes sting with... something. "That can't be true. Your family members are all stronger than I am."

"That's not what I mean." He slid down and turned to his side so that we were facing each other and trailed his fingers down my arm, leaving a wave of heat with his touch. "I'm talking in here." He lightly touched my temple. "And here." His hand pressed against my heart. "You're the one who survived living with that monster." The irony of Orin, who actually turned into a monster, calling my father one wasn't lost on me. "You ran off with me when you barely knew me."

"Which was probably stupid."

The corner of his mouth twitched. It was a decision that I'd never regret. "Probably. But you took a leap of faith. You put that faith in me and I'll never do anything to ruin it. You almost gave yourself to that man just so that you wouldn't be pushed off on someone else. You were taking that decision in your own hands instead of leaving it with your father." My face flared with embarrassment. That hadn't been my finest moment. Trying to be intimate with a man I considered my friend hadn't been my smartest idea, either, but it had pushed Orin into finally confessing his feelings for me. "You faced a pack of werewolves and fought them off. If that's not strength, I don't know what is."

"That was only because I didn't want Karina to be hurt," I protested. Also, I hadn't been thinking clearly or maybe I wouldn't have done it.

"Exactly. You are fiercely protective, even when outmatched. Your heart is stronger than anything else." He squeezed me to him, wrapping those arms around me so that I could let out a sigh. If I was in his arms, I was safe and protected. "You'll be able to weather this as well."

"I'm glad you believe that," I said against his chest.

"I know it." Once his arms relaxed, he still didn't let me go far. "And I think we should visit your aunt again tomorrow." Before I could protest, he added, "She has the answers that you want. That we need. There's no other way."

And that was how it was it decided that I'd return to my aunt the next day. The aunt who'd told me that my grandmother had been a banshee. The family dynamics, I still wasn't clear about, but she was the only person I'd be able to ask.

That night, I actually slept more than I thought I would and woke up ready to learn more about my mother and this new ability that I apparently had. If others had learned to control it, I would too, but in my sleep, I'd also decided that Orin had been right when he'd said that I should look at it like a... not a gift—that wasn't the right word, though it was the one he'd used—but an opportunity.

Control would be key though. I couldn't watch the death of every person who bumped into me. I wasn't strong enough for that.

Maybe in time I could be but right now, after everything we'd been through... I just couldn't.

After breakfast, we left to go to Audrey's house again. This time, Orin insisted that Roman and Karina have a day for themselves. He'd call them if he needed them. Given that telephones weren't everywhere, I assumed it'd be a wolf call of some kind.

Reluctantly, they agreed.

"I was hoping you'd come back," Audrey said when she opened the door. She looked out into the sunlight shining down onto an unusually warm morning. "How about we take a walk in the park? We can talk there."

"That sounds nice."

Orin and I were waiting on the front walk for her when he said, "Do you wonder why she doesn't want us in the house today?"

It hadn't occurred to me she had a particular reason, so no. Instead, she came out before I could answer.

The park was on the next block. It was beautiful with its greenery which in the coming months would be covered in snow. We didn't get a lot of snow back home, but I'd seen pictures.

"You want to ask questions," she said. It wasn't phrased as a question.

Orin trailed behind us, but I knew he could hear every word and likely, Audrey knew it too.

"Tell me about my mother," I said quietly. "I know it's not a question, but I know nothing of her."

A smile appeared on Audrey's face and then it was as if she were looking into another time. "Your mother was funny and beautiful. Just a small slip of a thing like you. You have her hair and her eyes. She was the most beautiful among us. Highly sought after as a mate." She took a breath before continuing. "We had no contact with my mother's side of the family. After the curse... how could we? So we grew up as wolf shifters."

"But you knew... about the other side?"

She nodded. "It wasn't something we thought about often, given that it was never going to be a factor. None of us ever considered we'd spill the blood of a family member, so there wasn't anything to worry about. But yes. We grew up knowing that side existed."

"Is that why you left?"

"Not exactly." We turned on the path, which allowed me to see that Orin was still right there with us, just ten feet behind. "As the population declined more, things weren't safe for us anymore." She shook her head. "The marriages were no longer love matches or even mate matches."

"What do you mean? I thought you found your mate and that was it."

She chuckled quietly. "No. That's not exactly right. Most found their mates and married, that's true, but finding your mate doesn't guarantee you want to spend your life with that person. There is such a thing as rejecting your mate. Actually, your mother rejected her mate."

"Really?"

She nodded and slipped her arm through mine so that we were walking arm in arm. "She did. She didn't want the universe telling her whom she'd spend the rest of her life with. However, once she'd rejected that mate, it was like open season on her. The men saw it as an opportunity to force her to mate with them. They needed babies and that meant they needed the women. Some had started to mate with human women; however, those babies don't always shift."

"Is that why I never have? My human side is winning out?"

She furrowed her brows. "No. With you, that's not the case."

A lump formed in my throat. "Does that mean I'll still shift one day?"

"No." She stopped and turned to me. "Your wolf is dormant. My children's wolves are dormant. If you haven't shifted yet, you won't. No one is exactly sure why, but we think it's because you're not full wolf. You have that little bit of banshee that has become dominant. Without talking to the pack, I don't know for sure." She began walking again.

"Your children?" I asked gently. "How old are they."

"Not much younger than you."

"Where are they?" Because as far as I could tell, they weren't around here.

She smiled as if a lovely memory crossed her mind. "They're both away at college. Twenty and eighteen."

College... what a dream and they were living it.

"And you don't talk to your pack?"

"No. And I can't even for you."

"What would happen if you did?"

"I left the pack. Turned my back on them and that would mean death if I went back. I can't risk that."

"I would never ask you to."

There were probably hundreds of questions that I had, but most of them Orin might've been able to answer. Right now, my mother was my priority since Audrey was the only person who could answer those.

"Did my mother shift? Did you?"

"Yes. I haven't for a very long time because it would be a way for the pack to find me. Your mother did try to shift when she was younger, but when we were teenagers, she stopped, insisting she didn't want to and wouldn't if she could."

"You mean you don't have to?"

"You don't. I'm sure your shifter can explain this." She glanced back at Orin. "You can fight it. It's not... comfortable, but you get used to the nagging urge always being there."

"Was she happy growing up?"

Audrey smiled. Once again, her eyes had a far-off look to them, as if she were seeing another time. "She was. Thora was one of the happiest children. She and I were carefree for a long time."

"Was she older than you?"

Her brows furrowed. "We were twins. Did Henry not tell you anything about her?"

"No." I shook my head slowly then took a deep breath. "We weren't allowed to discuss her. I only have a single picture of her. I think... I think he blamed me for her death."

"You are absolutely not to blame." She stopped again. "That's something the pack was dealing with. Probably still is, given that they came after you so that they could mate you. Our pack introduced humans to try to help perk up the numbers, but it wasn't working. Not everyone shifted—"diluted blood," the leaders called it. But shifter women were dying during childbirth for a while before your mother had you."

"Does that mean I won't be able to have children? You did."

"Yes. But I chose a husband, not a mate. He's human, though he knows all about this life. I don't know if that was what made the difference, but it might be a factor. If you're wondering if you will be able to have children with your shifter... I can't answer that."

That wasn't exactly the answer that I wanted. It wasn't that I was in a rush to have children with Orin, but it was something I wanted. With the other men I'd been promised to, I'd hoped that they were sterile. Now, knowing that I might give Orin a child and not be there to raise it with him... Well, I'd already known that, but hearing it from her was different.

"How did your father treat you growing up?" she asked once we were walking again.

"Not well," I answered honestly. "He was mean, harsh, and had a billion rules that I had to follow or else."

"Or else what, Elizabeth?" she asked urgently. "Did he hit you?"

I swallowed hard then nodded. "He did give me a smack now and then." I swore Orin growled quietly behind us. "I wouldn't say that I was beaten. I was just... there. An annoyance for him to take care of. I thought it was because I'd killed my mother and he'd loved her so much that he couldn't stand to look at me. Especially since I looked like her, judging by the picture I had." I shrugged. "Or maybe it was that I didn't look like him. I don't know."

Audrey snorted. "Why would it bother him that you didn't look like him?"

"I don't know. He was always so focused on how things appeared to everyone else. I was to be the most well-behaved child. Never doing anything that could shine a bad light on him. He wanted me to be pure so that he could make the best match. He wanted me trained in running the house so that I'd be the best wife and no one could complain. It was... exhausting and awful."

We were on our third loop around the park when I realized that I'd been so focused on what she was saying that I didn't ask if she'd like to sit. But since she didn't say anything, I didn't, either.

"The first man that he chose for me... wasn't a nice man. He wasn't nice to women in general and I knew it'd be a miserable experience. When he disappeared, my father chose another who was much better as far as being nice went, but he'd also been the man my best friend had hoped to marry before her parents had chosen her match. It hurt her feelings, but she understood that I had no say it in."

"The first man disappeared?" She glanced over her shoulder at Orin. There was nothing that could make me tell her that Orin had killed Noah Underwood when he'd gone to scare the man away from me. Nor would I tell her that Orin had paid a lot of money to ensure that my father would leave us alone.

"He did."

"What I don't understand, Elizabeth, is why your father was so harsh. He seemed like a very decent man when I met him."

My eyes widened. "You met him?"

"Of course I did. When your mother did. I was

also in town until your mother married him because we felt it was for the best not to be together. It was the last time that I saw her or spoke to her because it was too dangerous. We only exchanged letters rarely."

"But they had a courtship, right? You knew him for a long time."

She shook her head. "I didn't. They didn't have a long courtship. Actually, they married just weeks after meeting."

My mouth parted in surprise. That kind of hasty action wasn't something that I'd expected from my father. "He fell in love with her that quickly?"

"That's what your mother thought. And she was pregnant, so she didn't have a lot of choices."

My steps faltered and I thought I was going to fall, but Orin was there, catching me. Once he righted me on my feet, I asked, "What do you mean? She was pregnant when she got married?"

"Yes." She cocked her head to the side. "Henry Davis isn't your father, Elizabeth."

I stepped back, again, Orin there to keep me from falling as my blood turned cold in my veins.

If Henry Davis wasn't my father, then who was?

Chapter Seven

THE MAN who had raised me after my mother's death wasn't my father, even though he'd acted with a heavy hand and hadn't been required to.

Why hadn't he just sent me off to an orphanage and been done with me? Instead, he'd made my life as miserable as possible.

I had questions and wanted answers.

"Elizabeth?" Orin's voice was quiet in my ear, as if he were afraid someone would overhear him say my name. Probably he meant it for me to know that he was close.

"Why did he do all of those things, then?" I cried, the tears threatening to fall. Tears of relief, maybe? I didn't know.

"Lizzie." Orin began moving me off the sidewalk

where I'd stopped. "Sit down." Then I was sitting on a bench. He looked at Audrey. "Do you mind taking a break?"

"Not at all." She rushed over and sat beside me, not a single strand of her blonde hair out of place. "I'm sorry, Elizabeth. Honestly, I'm surprised you didn't already know. Your mother said she was going to tell you everything if she survived the birth." Her voice cracked on *survived*. In that moment, I was reminded that Audrey had lost her sister as much as I'd lost my mother. "She swore she was going to write a journal for you in case she didn't. Did you not receive the journal?"

I shook my head. "There is one. My f-father has it. I stole it from his office and read every single thing. It's how I found you, but then I gave it back."

"Then there must be another one." She glanced at Orin, who was squatted down beside me. "Or she didn't get a chance to write it, though I doubt that. She was adamant that it'd be the first thing she did. Maybe you could still find it." She rubbed my back the way you would soothe a toddler.

"What can you tell me?" I moved closer to her so that Orin could sit on the other side of me. It didn't seem like this conversation would be ending soon and I wanted him close. This was almost too much information to process all at once.

"There's a lot I can tell you," she conceded. "Though I wish you could read it in your mother's words." Audrey took a deep breath and then placed her hand over mine, the connection creating a wave of trust and at this point, given what I was learning, I wondered if that was a natural thing or if she could somehow affect my emotions.

"Your mother was already pregnant when she met Henry Davis," she began. "We were running from our family when she met him. He came from money, something Thora had never really cared about, but that money would equal security and protection for the both of you. If she were to live as a human, no one would ever know." Her blue eyes met mine. "It would've been easy for her to do. We didn't have the banshee inside of us and the wolf was dormant. Even when we lived in the pack, it had been like we were outsiders or humans, anyway."

"I can't imagine that the pack was too accepting of you if you couldn't shift," Orin added, making Audrey flinch ever-so-slightly.

"They weren't." But she wasn't going to elaborate on that because she continued about my father. "When she met Henry, I was there. He said she was the prettiest woman he'd ever seen, which she was. She and I may have been identical in almost every way, but somehow, she was prettier."

"How can that be true?" I asked, given that this was the first time I was hearing that they were identical twins.

"Her personality. She was so open and smiled all the time. I wasn't and didn't," she said. Even now, I realized that she hadn't smiled often in the short time we'd been together, but I'd thought that was because there wasn't much to smile about. "At first, Thora wasn't going to tell him that she was pregnant. She was going to allow him to think that you were his so that he'd always protect you the way she thought he would her."

"Guilt won out?" Orin asked and I was thankful. With everything she was telling me, I didn't know what questions to ask or where to lead the conversation. But Orin needed this information as much as I did.

"Guilt won out. She didn't want to lie when he was so in love with her or at least cared so deeply about her. But it turned out that he was looking for a beautiful woman to adorn his arm. To make him look good."

"That sounds like my father..." But he wasn't my

father at all. I raised my eyes to Orin, who was watching me closely. "That's probably why he treated me the way he did. Why he wanted to push me off on someone else as quickly as possible. He may have waited until I turned twenty-one this year, but he'd been planning since I was sixteen."

"If he knew," Audrey began, "why wouldn't he have just tossed you aside? Banished you from his house?"

A low rumble came from Orin's chest. It wasn't loud and I wasn't sure anyone else would've heard it. "Because he could get something for her."

Nodding, I turned back to my aunt. "It would have looked bad if the girl everyone thought was his daughter didn't marry well or wasn't taken care of. It's the only reason a man like him would've even kept me as a baby. Everyone had to already think I was his. What was he going to do? Tell society that he'd married a whore who'd gotten pregnant before being married?"

Even I couldn't believe those words had come out of my mouth, but it was the way my father would've seen it.

Audrey's jaw tightened. "She wasn't a whore. She was in love. She hadn't been with anyone other than your real father before she met Henry."

I shook my head and swallowed hard. "I wasn't saying that she was. But my father absolutely would've seen it that way if she'd told him she was already pregnant."

"Your real father and Thora had a ceremony between them. There weren't witnesses, so it wouldn't have been legal either way, but to them, their hearts were married."

So my mother had found love in her life. There was a pressure weighing down on my shoulders that suddenly lifted. The life I'd imagined she'd led before I'd been born wasn't pleasant and it was all based off how my father had treated me. Now, I knew that she'd had a great love of her life and for reasons I may never understand, they couldn't be together, which was how she'd ended up with my father. For all I knew, my adoptive father had treated her well when they'd been together. I just couldn't imagine it.

"That's probably why he focused on making a match for you that would benefit his business," Orin said quietly. "Instead of caring what you wanted, he wanted something for himself."

"What does that mean?" Audrey asked.

"He made matches that would significantly increase his wealth or business in one way or another. It wasn't about what was good for me, but what was good for him."

"I'm sorry he did that to you, Elizabeth." The sympathy in her voice was almost too much to take. "How did you two end up together, then? There's no way a man like that would've allowed it, no matter how much money the Vilkatas family had."

"He paid my father ten thousand dollars for me," I admitted without shame. It had gotten my father to leave us alone.

Audrey sat up straight. "That is a sizable sum."

"It was worth it," Orin told her immediately. He'd tried to sway any guilt I had about him having to put out such a large amount of money just to keep my father from trying to take me back. I wasn't going to dwell on that any longer, but it was nice to hear him say that he didn't regret it.

"It's roughly what we thought he'd profit from my marriage to Noah or Bradley." That was where I'd decided the number had come from. It didn't matter if it was true or not.

Audrey patted my hand. "It seems Orin is a good man." Then she leaned in and whispered, "Even if he is a werewolf."

Orin's loud laugh broke the tension that I'd been

feeling this entire morning. This was all almost too much to take.

My father wasn't my father. My real father might still be out there and I had no idea who I was.

Wait. No. I did.

I was Elizabeth Vilkatas, Orin's wife. And happy to be that. Everything else didn't matter.

"How did you know?" I asked her, but she narrowed her eyes in confusion. "That he's a were-wolf? We didn't tell you."

Now she gave me a genuine smile and I imagined this was what it'd be like to sit next to my mother. Given that they were identical twins, this was as close as I'd ever get.

"The wolf in me may never have emerged, but that doesn't mean I haven't perfected a few senses on my own. Some of the traits are still there." She cocked her head to the side. "For example, I know that his brother isn't far. I can hear him and the woman coming this way."

Now I furrowed my brows. "How did you know it's his brother?"

"I heard him outside of my house the first day you came to me. They sound too similar not to be brothers."

"How do you know all of this?" I asked. "If you

and my mother didn't speak after her marriage, how do you know everything that you do?"

Audrey sat up taller, almost as if pride were washing over her then she looked at the watch on her wrist. "I have all of her letters, my dear. If you'd like, we can go back to my house and I'll give them to you. If you can't find the journal she meant for you, at least you would have those."

That perked my interest right up. Until this point, everything had sounded like bad news. I wasn't my father's daughter. He hadn't loved my mother, anyway. My mother couldn't be with the man she truly loved.

But being able to read my mother's own thoughts, the things she'd wanted her sister to know... that was good news indeed.

"I would love that."

Roman and Karina didn't approach us. Instead, they watched from afar, though it seemed a silent conversation took place between the brothers, as it often did.

We returned to her house, though this time she let us inside unlike when we'd arrived. Whatever had been in there that she hadn't wanted us to see was clearly gone. Audrey disappeared up her stairs, which gave me my first moment alone in a while with Orin.

"How are you handling all of this?" he asked as he pulled me into his arms.

"I should ask you that," I said. "After all, you're the one who's discovered your wife isn't who you thought she was."

His brows pinched together. "Do you think for a second that who your father is had any bearing on my marrying you? It didn't. I don't care what your bloodlines are, outside of it being a reason that the Balodis pack isn't going to leave us alone. Knowing will help me protect you."

"And help me protect you?" I asked. "Given that I should now be able to warn you if you're in danger if I can figure out how to control this. It's not like I see death at every turn but that could mean I won't see it when I need to. I need to be able to call on it."

"I'm not afraid of danger," he countered.

My stomach tightened. He'd already told me he'd die to keep me safe. Something I didn't want to happen. "I know that, but if you know where it's coming from, you should be able to protect yourself and your brothers better."

"That much is true." He took a breath and parted his lips, like there was more he wanted to say, but

Audrey came down the stairs before he had the chance.

"Here they are." She handed me a brown box that was heavier than I'd thought it'd be. "These are all of them. I never understood why I kept them, given that if they were ever found by my family, they'd be able to track you down and the danger that would bring. I just couldn't throw them away." She gave me a warm smile and rested her hands on my shoulders. "And now I know I kept them to give them to you."

With tears welling up in my eyes, I said, "Thank you."

"You're very welcome. And know that you were always loved. At least by your mother and by me. I may not have met you until now, but you were always in my thoughts."

I swallowed hard and tried to come up with something to say to that, but there weren't any words that would fully convey what I was feeling.

"You understand that we likely won't be able to come back." That was Orin, back to business, taking over where I couldn't.

She smiled again. "Yes. But I met my niece at least this once. I can go to my grave a grateful woman."

That was when I realized that she had touched me several times and I hadn't had any fear of what I was going to see. It was like I'd forgotten that I could see people's deaths.

At least for the moment.

Now, I was anxious to get back to the hotel to learn about my mother.

Chapter Eight

It was likely the last time I'd see my aunt. Being there was a danger to her since her pack, the Balodis pack, was still after me. If I led them to her and something happened, I'd never forgive myself. So far, there had been no flashes of her death when she'd touched me, but I began to wonder... was that why she'd been touching me in the first place? So that I'd see her death if it was coming?

I wished I had asked her before we'd left her house.

As soon as Orin and I stepped onto the walkway, Roman and Karina were there walking with us. They joined right behind us as if they'd been there the entire time.

"Find out anything new?" Roman asked, but I didn't get the feeling he was asking me.

"Yes. A lot." Orin glanced over his shoulder. "We'll talk about it later."

That seemed to satisfy Roman for now.

Once we were back at the hotel, Roman and Karina wanted to get lunch. If I were honest with them, I didn't think I could take a single bite, so I told them as much. All I could think about was reading my mother's letters.

"I'll come with you," Orin told me.

"No." I placed a hand on his chest to stop him. "You have to be starving. Stay with them. Eat. All I'm going to do it sit and read these letters. This way, I can fill you in when you're done." Then I glanced at his brother. "And you can fill them in on what we found out so far."

"I don't have to tell them everything," he said quietly, though I knew he offered that for me. There were things in my past that some would find distasteful, but there wasn't anything I could do about that and keeping his family in the dark would only put them in more danger.

"No," I told him. "You can tell them everything. I'm not embarrassed and I don't think your family will judge my mother for getting pregnant before she was married." Given that he'd told me the wolves lived differently, even having sex with numerous partners before getting married. It was casual, he'd told me. They didn't live by the rules of the society I was raised in.

"They won't."

Orin quickly brushed the palm of his hand over my cheek like he was going to cup it, but then he dropped it. He might've been comfortable with affection in public, but I was still warming up to it. If he had his way, he'd kiss me in a very inappropriate way even if everyone were watching. He didn't because I was still nervous about those things.

"I'll take you up to the room," he told me, taking my hand.

"No. Just give me the key and I'll go up." I held out my hand and when he didn't immediately give me the keys, I sighed. "I can get myself up to the room. You've got to be hungry and you need to talk to your brother. Orin, I'll be fine."

His jaw was tense as he handed the keys. I pushed to my toes and kissed him on the cheek. What each of us had done was a big step. "Thank you."

As I left him to go to our room, I knew Orin would watch me until he couldn't anymore.

It was ridiculous. No one knew we were in Boston right now, so this was the most freedom we'd had since we'd met. And I couldn't expect to be with Orin every moment of my life. Normally, I would've taken the stairs, but right now, I really wanted to get to my room and dive into these letters. There weren't many, but I wanted to consume them immediately. Because I was in a hurry, I took the lift.

Once I was in my room, I sat in the chair by the window and took a deep breath. These letters had been written by my mother and this was the closest I'd ever be to her. There were only six.

The first letter didn't tell me much. It was a basic check-in to make sure that Audrey had gotten to Boston without any problem. There were also a few lines that seemed to be answering questions that had been asked in another letter, likely one that Audrey had sent her when she'd arrived.

In my mind, this was the response to the first letter that Audrey had sent my mother since Audrey would've known my mother's address. It was what made the most sense.

There was another letter talking about how weird it was to be pregnant. The fact that a tiny human was inside her and that each day she tried not to think about the fact that her surviving my birth wasn't likely. According to her, the way the pack birthrate had dropped due to the women dying during the process, she was worried about it.

She wasn't scared, though. She was adamant that whatever happened would happen and as long as I was taken care of, it'd be worth it. My mother talked about me being conceived in love and as long as that love was able to make it into the world, she'd accept her fate.

A tear ran down my cheek at the thought of my mother willingly giving her life for mine. She had been the first to do that, but not the last. Memories of Phillip flooded my mind, but the two of them together were too much grief for me to handle, so he had to wait.

After carefully folding the second letter and returning it to the envelope, I opened the third.

Dear Audrey,

As my stomach grows, so do many feelings inside me. I'm so excited to meet this little one, but I'm also worried that it won't be for long. Henry has been an absolutely doting husband. Even though he knows the truth, he insists that he'll take care of the baby and me for the rest of our lives. It's only been a few months and I'm not sure if he's in love with me, but he does care for me. We're creating a life together. A life he says he's always wanted.

If I don't survive this, at least I know that this baby will be taken care of and loved. And no one will ever find her.

I trust you to keep all my secrets.

Your sister,

Thora

I swallowed hard as I put that letter away. My mother had thought that I was going to be loved and cared for. It was as if she hadn't really known my father at all.

Or my first suspicions were true. He'd loved my mother and her death had crippled him emotionally. Maybe he hadn't had anything left to give. Yet he'd still kept his promise. He'd made sure I'd been taken care of. Maybe that had been all he could do.

Feeling bad for my father wasn't something I'd seen happening ever, let alone today.

The next two letters were much of the same. Updates. Barely a mention of their family or what was happening. And not another word about her being worried she wouldn't be there to raise me.

I didn't know how you could miss someone you'd never met, but I was missing her right now.

It wasn't until the last letter that I found something more. I'd keep and treasure every one of them and probably read them a thousand more times. But that last one, that was where the real information was. Or at least how I would find everything out.

Dearest Audrey,

With the arrival of this baby imminent, I've decided to send this letter in case it's the last one that I send. I know this baby is a girl. Don't ask me how, but I do. I'm going to name her Elizabeth, after our mother. It's the only thing of our family I can give her and the only good thing that I could want.

You know everything that happened with Coltar already. You know what he is. You know what his family is. I'd like you to write down everything you know and keep it safe in case my daughter ever comes looking for it. Make her ask!! Don't just offer it up to her. I wouldn't want to shock her unless she knows about our world already. It's possible she may find you just for information about me—if I'm not here to give it myself. But I want a record of it somewhere and you're the only person I can fully trust with my secrets, this information, and how to handle my daughter in my absence. I wish I could leave her to you, but I know that it's not a smart idea, considering our family will never stop looking for us.

Coltar was a good man from a bad family.

Nothing more. If he had been anything other than what he was, we would've had a good life.

It's like I can see my daughter in my mind's eye already. She's beautiful and looks like us. I wish I could explain it, but you're well aware that there are too many things that we can't explain. I've already started feeling the first pains of labor, which is why it was so urgent to write this letter.

I love you, Audrey. You are the best sister anyone could ask for.

Please stay safe.

All my love,

Thora

A sob ripped from my chest. My mother had already been in labor with me and had chosen to write to her sister, as if she'd known she wouldn't survive. More than that, she'd wanted me to know about my father. My real father, not Henry Davis.

I wiped away a tear that was streaming down my cheek as the door to my room opened.

"Orin, I just finished—"

"Not Orin, sweetheart."

My heart thudded to a stop for a split second before taking off like a racing horse. My gaze flew up to see a large man with blond hair, not unlike mine—

though his was short and well styled—shutting the door behind him.

I jumped to my feet. "You have the wrong room," I told him, hoping this was all just a mistake.

"I have the right room. My pack has been looking for you. Imagine my surprise when I saw you on the street in Boston." His chin was too big for his face, chiseled out of marble or something equally as hard. His broad chest reminded me of how large the men in the Balodis pack were. Or the men in Vilkatas pack.

"Stay away from me," I warned, holding my hand up as if I had the power to do something. "I'll scream."

"Go ahead. Your husband and his brother are three doors down. They won't hear you even with their wolf hearing."

I didn't know if that was true or not—could the wolf hearing work differently inside than out—but I wasn't going to take the chance of using that energy and it not even working. Mental note: Ask Orin how far away he can hear.

Slowly, I put the letter down on the table beside the chair I'd been sitting in, suddenly thankful that I'd decided to wear trousers today, even though I'd received many strange looks by doing so. Trousers for women were catching on, but we weren't there yet.

"What do you want?" I asked.

He ran his tongue over his bottom lip and said, "You know exactly what I want."

My stomach turned and I suddenly felt nauseous.

To breed me. That was what the Balodis pack wanted. It didn't make sense, honestly. Orin had said they were probably desperate for anyone with a morsel of the Balodis blood, but even if they got me, only one could mate with me.

Or, as Karina had reminded me... only one *at a time* could.

My head was suddenly light, but I wasn't going to be a helpless damsel in distress right now. Without Orin or his family around me, I had to fend for myself.

When he moved closer, I moved to the side in the hope of getting myself closer to the door.

"Now, there's no one to protect you." He lunged.

As hard as I tried, I wasn't fast enough to get out of his reach. His big hands wrapped around my arms. I pushed, pulled, and flailed to get away from him and when that didn't work, I used my nails to claw down his face.

He dropped his hold on me as he yelled. I bolted for the door. I'd just gotten my hand on the knob when his chest slammed into my back.

"You're not going anywhere except with me."

"Let me go." I pushed back. He had me so tightly against the door that it took all of my air to say those words. Black spots were floating around the edges of my vision. I had to do something.

Mustering up all the anger I had, all of the desire within me for him to go away, I wiggled myself around so that I was facing him, dug my thumbs into his eye sockets, and pushed.

This man was a hundred times stronger than me, but an energy flowed through me that I'd never felt before. He fell to his knees, his yell getting quieter and quieter and then he... fell to the ground with a loud *thud*.

It was enough for me to slip out the door and run.

I hurried down the stairs, constantly looking back to see if he was following, but so far, he wasn't.

I bumped into three people trying to get to the restaurant before I heard, "Lizzie?" And Orin was rushing toward me. "Elizabeth, what happened?"

"A man," I gasped. I'd been running so quickly that I didn't think I'd taken in a breath. "A man came into our room." It took another breath before I could continue, but anger was already boiling through my husband.

"What's going on?" Roman demanded, suddenly beside me with Karina on the other side.

"A Balodis came into our room." Having them around me calmed the fear. "He came in when I was reading the letters. Said I was going with him."

"Stay here," Orin demanded, then he took off in a hurry toward the stairs.

"Karina, stay here with her. He won't do anything with this many people around." Then Roman was running after his brother.

Karina wrapped an arm around my shoulders and pulled me close to her. "I think Orin had a heart attack when he saw you running with some of your hair wild. He had to have imagined the worst."

"It almost was the worst."

"How did you get away?"

"I don't know," I told her honestly. "I got my hands on him and jammed my thumbs into his eyes... but he fell over, as if he'd died. He was still there when I came down here."

"Don't worry, then." She rubbed a hand up and down my arm. "Roman and Orin will handle him."

We waited for one of the men to come back

down and the more time that passed, the more agitated Karina became.

"We should go check on them," I told her.

She shook her head. "Roman said to stay here."

"Karina. Don't you want to make sure your husband is all right?"

She looked at me and her mouth opened like she was going to protest, but then she snapped it shut. "OK. We'll go, but you stay close to me."

I agreed and we headed for the stairs. She took them slower than the guys had, but soon enough, we were at my room and the door was slightly ajar. She slowly reached out her hand when the door flew open, causing the both of us to jump.

"Jesus Christ, Roman." She slapped at her husband. "You scared the hell out of us."

He grinned. "We could hear you coming." Then he waved us in.

Immediately, I want to Orin's side as he gazed down at a small drop of blood on the carpet.

"It was definitely a Balodis," he said.

"I told you that, but how do you know for sure?"

He pointed at the carpet. "The blood. I can smell it. What did he want?"

"Me, of course. It's what they always want."

"We should go to the packhouse," Roman told

him, whatever that meant. "It's the only place we can make sure she's safe right now."

Orin nodded as his brother spoke. "We'll leave now."

"No. Wait." I grabbed his hand in mine to stop him. "I have to see Audrey."

"We can't, Elizabeth. We have to get you somewhere safe."

"Please," I begged. "It will probably be the last time I see her and I have to get a couple more answers."

He and Roman had one of their silent conversations before he finally said, "Fine. But you have to be quick."

I would be.

All I needed was whatever she'd written down about my father.

Chapter Nine

Orin packed our bags while I put the letters carefully back into the box that Audrey had given me to them in. Then I pushed them into my suitcase and covered them with clothing as if they'd be damaged in the trip.

I didn't know where the packhouse was or what to expect when we got there, but for now, my focus was on my aunt.

She wouldn't tell me certain things because my mother had asked her to wait for me to ask. It made sense and it filled me with a warmth that the mother who had protected me before I'd been born had protected me after she died. My only guess was that my mother knew how overwhelming all of this was and how it could overtake me.

What if I'd come to my aunt without knowing about wolves? What if I'd only known a little?

Roman and Karina took our bags. As I was about to protest, Orin said, "It's the only way we can go see your aunt."

Which immediately made me give in.

It struck me as odd that Roman wasn't coming with us, but Karina walked on one side of me while Orin was on the other. I wanted to know where Roman had gone but wanted to get to my aunt more. We took a taxi which dropped us at her corner.

"Minutes, Elizabeth," Orin told me then glanced around. "You have minutes and then I'm going to have to get you out of there. If there's one Balodis, there's more. We can't lead them to your aunt."

"Of course. I don't want that." But sadly, I hadn't considered it, either. "Are you coming?"

He shook his head. "Karina and I are going to stay out here to make sure no one tries to get in that house." He kissed my forehead. "Be quick."

I ran to my aunt's house and banged my closed fist against the door. It only took two times before she pulled the door open. I pushed inside without saying a word.

"Elizabeth? I thought you were leaving?" She stood back and shut the door.

"I read the letters, Audrey. My mother asked you to write everything out about my father. My real father. She wanted you to wait until I asked for it. I'm asking."

"She did want me to wait," she confirmed. "Thora had told me that she wrote the truth about your Henry Davis not being your father and referred you to me in the journal. The one you haven't seen. She thought if you came to me, you probably wouldn't know the things you do about wolves or any other paranormal things." Audrey scurried into the room opposite the one we'd sat in and I followed. She opened the drawer of a desk and pulled out an envelope. "This is everything, but, Elizabeth, this is just for you to know. You can't go looking for him."

"Why not?" We were on a clock and any notion of not being blunt was long gone.

She watched me, considering her options.

"Audrey, one of the Balodis just attacked me in our hotel room. We are leaving. This is your only chance to help me understand my mother and where I came from."

She sighed. "Your father is an incubus, Elizabeth. Do you know what that means?" I shook my head slowly. If I hadn't known what a banshee was, I sure didn't know what an incubus was. "It's a male demon who likes to have... intercourse with women. Human women."

"My mother wasn't human."

"No, she wasn't. That's why they were able to fall in love. Your mother, whether it be the wolf or the banshee—none of his *charms* worked on us. Or rather none of his demon charms. Other charms definitely worked on your mother." She took a deep breath. "We ran because of everything I've already told you, but also, we were worried that the pack wouldn't accept you with your incubus part. When an incubus produces an offspring, it's said the women birth witches and other demons, and you never knew which you're going to get."

"So I'm a witch? A demon?"

"No. Or I don't think so. Because of your mother's blood, you are something else entirely. So either our pack would kill you for being you, use you the way they are trying to now, or his family would come for you. Either way, we ran. Since we didn't shift, they couldn't track us through normal wolf ways."

"Thank you, Aunt Audrey." I threw myself into her arms for a hug. When I pulled back, I asked, "Is he still alive? My father?"

She closed her eyes and held them there for several seconds before opening them. "He was last I knew, but that was decades ago. He took a wife, last I heard. Had kids."

"I have siblings?"

"You did but currently? I don't know, Elizabeth. It's been so long."

The loud pounding on the door made both of us jump. "It's Orin," she said before opening the door.

"Lizzie, we have to go. Roman's here."

I looked back at my aunt and said, "Thank you. I hope to see you again someday."

"Write to me."

And then I was hurrying down her front steps until coming to a stop next to a car. "What is this?" I asked.

"It's how we're getting to the packhouse." Orin yanked the door open and nudged me inside.

Roman was speeding off before I had a chance to ask anything else. "Where did you get this?" I asked him.

"Borrowed," he said, but when I glanced at Karina she shook her head and mouthed, *Stolen*.

"You stole this car?" The outrage in my voice filled the interior of the vehicle.

Orin turned so that he could look at me. "We didn't have a choice. We couldn't be trapped on a train and one doesn't go where we're going, anyway. Sit back. We've got a bit of a ride ahead of us."

We were out of the city before I decided to tell them everything from the letters and what Audrey had said. And I told them everything. Even about me being part demon. They took it much better than I had.

"What does it mean, though?" I asked. "If I'm what... a wolf, banshee, and an incubus. What does that make me?"

"All of those things," Karina asked. "It doesn't matter. You're Elizabeth."

"What about..." I blew out a breath slowly. "Abilities. I saw that man die. That's something, right?"

Roman glanced worriedly at Orin and again it was like they were having a conversation I couldn't hear.

"That is something," Orin finally said. "And more talents may appear."

"Wait." Karina sat up straight in the seat. "Do you think that's what happened to the man in the hotel room? I've heard that an incubus has the power to drain energy. I always thought it was through sex, but what if it isn't? What if she did it with her hands?"

The silence in the car meant that everyone could

hear my heart thud in my chest. They probably could all hear it, anyway, but now I could hear it, too.

"It's possible," Orin finally admitted. "We'll have to test it once we're at the house."

Test it? How? I didn't think I wanted to know.

The emotion of the day set in and though it was mid-afternoon, I sat back and let the sway of the car rock me to sleep. Until I bolted upright with this cold feeling washing over me, like someone from the dead was trailing a hand down the bare skin of my arm.

"Stop," I yelled louder than I needed to.

Roman hit the brake pedal and the car skidded to a stop. He turned to me with wide eyes. "What?"

"I don't know," I told him while looking out one window after another. With no idea of how much time had passed and no idea where we were, I couldn't explain it.

"You yell like that, but you don't know?" Roman demanded, raising his voice enough to get a growl out of Orin.

"Watch it," Orin warned.

"Why? She scared the life out of me but has no idea why. Karina could've been killed."

"By what?" He gestured around. "This is a country road. There's nothing out here."

"It was a feeling," I told him. Karina sat up, leaning against the seat in front of her.

"A feeling?" Orin asked.

"It was like the hand of death itself was running down my arm. I don't know why, but you needed to stop."

Roman gave Orin an exasperated look.

Then Orin's head snapped to the right, his gaze going out the window. "Do you feel that?" he asked, but the question wasn't directed at me.

"Yeah," answered his brother.

Orin and Roman jumped out of the car. The windows were down, so we could hear everything, though it didn't all make sense. They headed toward a field that had been plowed recently but veered far enough that I couldn't see them anymore.

A horrible growling filled the air followed by something that sounded like a scream. My hand clenched the seat in front of me.

"What's going on?" I asked, but Karina was on high alert.

"They found something," she said quietly. It wasn't a whisper, exactly—more like she was distracted. "Shit," she said under her breath.

I was still getting used to hearing a woman swear.

Their kind was very different from my father's society.

Three heartbeats later, I finally saw Orin and Roman coming up toward the back of the car. Both were naked with their hands strategically placed over their most personal areas. I quickly checked to make sure no cars were coming and luckily, the nearest house that I could see was far enough away that the people there wouldn't know that these men were naked, if they saw them at all.

Karina sighed. "It's a wonder we ever get anything done."

I furrowed my brows. "What do you mean?"

She pointed at the men. "Look at them. Don't tell me he couldn't convince you to stay in bed all day."

Heat flared across my skin.

"Elizabeth." She smiled. "It's OK. We're going to the packhouse. It's a very open society. That doesn't mean we'll be talking about sexual things in front of everyone, but I'm your sister." She shrugged. "Or the closest you have to one, anyway. We can talk about these things."

"I don't..." I blew out a breath. "I don't know that I can."

She bumped my shoulder with hers. "We'll work on it. But I'm right, aren't I?"

I used everything I had to keep from smiling and it didn't work. Karina giggled beside me.

Orin absolutely could convince me to stay in bed with him all day. Seeing all of that golden skin on display as he walked back toward the car caused a burning deep inside me. One I didn't think would be quenched for a while.

The guys went to the back of the car, so I turned around quickly. Karina righted herself a lot less quickly.

"What're they doing back there?" I asked quietly, as if they wouldn't hear me.

"Getting new clothes, I would guess."

Yes. That made sense. They'd obviously shifted and torn the clothes from their bodies. Quickly, they were back in the car and Roman was driving as if nothing had happened.

Finally, Karina said, "You're really not going to tell us what happened?"

Roman groaned. "Of course I am. We were being followed. Now we aren't."

"You killed him?" I asked.

"Well..." He dragged the word out. "I technically

did not." Orin growled. "What? She asked the question."

I leaned up and laid my hand on Orin's shoulder. "You killed him?"

"Had to." He looked over his shoulder at me, those dark eyes still on fire from whatever they'd done out there. "He couldn't follow us to the packhouse."

And that was all the information I was going to get.

Twenty minutes later, we pulled down a dirt drive that made it look like we were heading into the forest. But the trees parted to a clearing with a large house in the middle of the woods. Not as big as my father's house, but much larger than Orin's.

"This is where most of us live," Orin said as we got out of the car. There were little kids running around and playing in front of the house and yelling coming from somewhere else.

"You grew up here?" I squinted up at him, the sunlight bright against his back.

"I did. I know these trees like the back of my own hand."

Roman chuckled. "We've all spent enough time in them."

"Come on." He put my hand in his to lead me to the house with Roman and Karina right behind us. Then he maneuvered me through the large entryway that had stairs going up one wall. Everything was well maintained, with a beautiful, lined wallpaper on the walls. I thought it was wallpaper. My father didn't like it, so we didn't have it, which meant I wasn't an expert.

We walked down a darker hallway and then entered the kitchen. For being so far out in the countryside, the kitchen was as modern as it could be. And huge, with an enormous table through another archway.

"What are you doing here?" Emmi asked as she came out from in front of the large stove to wrap her arms around Orin and then me. She repeated the same with Roman and Karina. "Why are you here?" Emmi's hair was back in a bun and her dark eyes were kind. They hadn't always been with me and I appreciated the warm welcome. I wouldn't get that from everyone here.

"Can we fill you all in at once?" Orin asked. "Dinner?"

That was when I realized we were inching closer to dinner and my stomach reminded me that I hadn't eaten lunch, either.

"Sounds like I better hurry it up." She tilted her

head toward me and the noise my stomach had just made. "You all go and freshen up. I'll get this ready and call everyone in. I assume it's not good news."

Boy, was she right.

Orin led me back out and up the stairs. It wasn't until the third door on the right that he stopped and brought me inside.

His room was large, much like mine had been at my father's house. His bed loomed over the room in the middle. Everything was dark wood and masculine colors. Very different from the room we shared at home.

"This was your room growing up?"

"It was." He sat on the edge of the bed and brought me between his legs.

"I can see you growing up here, but, Orin, everything here is dark and masculine. It's so different from our room at home. Is this what you like?"

He shook his head and then pressed his forehead to my chest. "I like what we have at home. You're there."

I pushed my fingers into his hair, making him sigh. "I love it when you touch me like this."

"Only like this?"

He propped his chin where his forehead had just been and looked up at me. "Not only like this."

I smiled down at him then cupped his hard jaw so that I could kiss him. It wasn't often I initiated things, but I wanted to be bold more often. More like Karina, I thought.

"We should get cleaned up," I said after bringing the kiss to an end.

"Hungry?"

"Yes," I told him. "I haven't eaten since breakfast."

"You know we're almost halfway back to our house. We could be there soon."

"But you said—"

"No. We're staying here at least for a few days, but I wanted you to know we're close to home."

"Isn't this your home?"

He wrapped his arms around my waist, his chest to my back, and dropped his chin to my shoulder. "It is right now because this is where you are, but no. *Our* home is my home." Then he kissed my shoulder. "I'm going to go get our bags."

Once he was back with our things, I quickly washed up and righted my hair. I couldn't believe I'd come into Emmi's house looking so disheveled. Orin cleaned up too. He still had tiny specks of blood on his arms.

"Ready?" he asked, probably because he knew, as

I did, that not everyone was going to be happy to see me. Him, yes. Me? Not so much.

He held my hand as he took me back downstairs to the kitchen that we'd passed through to get to the dining room. But he stopped short when he heard a voice.

"*She*'s here?" the woman asked with outrage. "Why are they here? I can't see her."

That was when I realized it was Diana asking the questions. Phillip's wife, who rightfully blamed me for his death. She turned and spotted Orin and me in the doorway.

"I could kill you," she said and her eyes told me she was absolutely serious.

Chapter Ten

ORIN MOVED me behind him so I could barely see Diana standing there with her strawberry-blonde hair pulled back away from her face and her dark eyes burning me. In my opinion, her anger was warranted. In Orin's, it wasn't.

"Stand down, Diana," Orin said, acting as my sentry by putting his body between her and me. I had no doubt she could kill me before she moved. "It wasn't her fault."

Diana looked away from him with shiny eyes, like she was about to cry. Phillip had been her husband—her mate—and he'd died protecting me for Orin. She had every right to blame me. If I could've done something... not been such a weak human, maybe he would have still been alive.

Diana's eyebrows shot up. "Not her fault, Orin? He died protecting a pathetic human. We don't do that."

Orin growled and started to take a step forward, but I put my hand on his arm to stop him. "Orin, don't." I stepped in front of him. "It's my fault," I told her. "I know that and I'm sorry. I'm so sorry and I wish I could do something to take away your pain."

Diana shook her head but didn't look at me. It was as if I weren't there at all. "I'm not going to sit here and eat dinner with her." She stomped over to her daughter, Ruby, who was happily playing with a rattle and had tiny wisps of strawberry-blonde curls around her ears. She was still a baby. One who would never know her father.

Then Diana snatched her out of the highchair she was in and trudged out of the room. Anything to get away from me.

Aras stood suddenly. I hadn't had a chance to take inventory of who from the family was here, but it was all of them. Aras had cut her chestnut hair since the last I'd seen her. It was a fashionable bob and made her look like she should be modeling the latest styles. She was tall and thin, could pull off the androgynous look that was so popular right now. I couldn't. My curves would never allow it. Her husband, Daniel, the oldest of the Vilkatas boys, gave her a nod of acknowledgement.

While she left, she took her son with her, and I took stock of who was left. Daniel, Roman, Ivan, and Orin all looked like brothers. They had the same dark hair and eyes. The differences were slight, though they didn't look like multiples. Daniel had the broadest shoulders. Orin was the tallest. Roman had the most muscles. Ivan was the thinnest yet still very strong, given the fact that he was a wolf.

Their wives couldn't have been more different. Diana was taller than me, but not the same as Aras and had the strawberry-blonde hair. Aras's hair was dark like her husband's, Karina was only slightly taller than me and had dark-blonde hair. Nell, Ivan's wife, had beautiful dark-brown hair that she still kept longer and curled. Much like me. Then I arrived with my curves and blonde hair that I hadn't cut short, as was the style.

I wasn't a wolf. Or rather, I hadn't known I was when I'd met Orin, and I'd done everything wrong with this family.

Or that was how it felt.

"Please sit down," Emmi said as she pointed to two seats near her. I didn't think putting us beside her had been an accident. Nor was the fact that Orin had me sit between his mother and him.

Emmi may not have wanted me for her child, but once she'd known I was who he wanted, she'd accepted me. His father, Anton... wasn't as sure. He'd accepted that I was Orin's wife and he'd protect me as he would any of the others, but deep down, I thought he was also still wary of me.

"Let's eat," Emmi said.

The sound of the silverware clanking as the dishes were passed from one person to another filled the air where the conversation hadn't yet. Orin offered whatever he had to me first and I took a little bit of everything, not intending to eat it all. There was roast beef with gravy, mashed potatoes, cooked carrots, and rolls with the most delicious butter. All things that had been served in my father's house. This was just served differently. The dishes were passed instead of held beside you by a servant. We all had large glasses of water instead of the bottles and bottles of wine that had been tableside at every dinner my father had had.

I preferred this.

"It'll just take some time," Karina told me. She and Roman were across from Orin and me. The table wasn't wide like what I was used to. Again, I preferred the hominess of this setup. It was warm and mostly inviting.

"I understand," I told her. Then, for the first time in front of his family, I said what I felt out loud. "I can't be upset with her for blaming me. I blame myself."

The noise came to a stop and Orin turned in his chair to face me. "I've told you that none of this is your fault."

"Is that true, though?" Ivan said, speaking for the first time, which earned him a scowl from my husband. "What? If not for her, Phillip would still be here, right?" Nell nodded beside him. "So doesn't that make it her fault?"

"No," Orin snapped. "It isn't her fault that the Balodis came after her."

Ivan held up a hand. "I didn't say that them coming after her was her fault, but if she could've kept her ass at home instead of going to the market—"

"I wanted to go to the market too," Karina told him, coming to my defense.

I wouldn't argue his point. He wasn't wrong. I'd wanted to be useful and I'd ended up costing their brother his life.

"You can handle yourself," Ivan countered.

Orin was about to counter him again when I said, "He's right." This brought everyone's attention to me and their arguing stopped. "He's right. I'll never forgive myself, so I don't expect others to forgive me. If I could do this whole thing over, I would. But I can't. I also can't make Orin leave me. I've tried." Another growl rumbled in his chest. "So this is where we are." I settled my gaze on Ivan. His eyes were so heated that I almost couldn't look directly at him, but for this, I would. "You don't have to forgive me. You don't have to like me. I understand. There's just nothing I can do about any of this."

At least that brought the arguing to an end and we finished dinner in silence.

"I'll help with dishes," I said as I brought my plate into the kitchen. Another thing that was different from how I'd grown up, but I was very comfortable with it. At home, now, with Orin, we did the dishes together. It was something normal in our lives.

"No," Orin answered for me. "We need to talk to my parents. I told them we'd meet them somewhere we could talk in private."

Oh. Right. Tell them that I was a mangy mutt that Orin had found on the side of the road. Not exactly something I wanted to tell them.

His parents were both tall and... sturdy, I guess I'd call it. They'd scared me when I'd first met them and I'd be lying if I said there wasn't something still there that reminded me of that fear. But they'd accepted me and acted accordingly. They also didn't seem to blame me for their son's death, something I'd never know how they dealt with.

"Don't worry," Karina said, taking my plate from me. "Roman and I have this."

Orin took my hand in his to lead me down the hall. There were so many doors, I had to wonder where they all led. I wasn't sure I'd explore this house on my own, though. Never knew when I'd run into Diana and what her anger would unleash at any given moment.

Once he and I were at the end of the hallway, Orin pushed the large, wooden door open, revealing a study or an office. I wasn't sure which. It could've been both.

Books lined the walls, so maybe it was their library.

"It's good to have the two of you here," Emmi said as she stood. This time, she wrapped her arms around me in a fierce hug. Anton grunted, which I thought meant he agreed, but he didn't stand. He didn't hug me and that was fine with me.

Emmi took her seat next to Anton on one couch while Orin brought me to the one on the other side so that we could both sit.

Anton began the conversation. "Roman said you have some things to tell us."

I swallowed hard as acid burned my stomach and although I didn't eat much, I wished I had eaten less because it was a brick right now.

"Yeah." Orin glanced at me, but I was more than happy to have him tell it. "Elizabeth found her mother's sister. As you discovered, her mother was a member of the Balodis pack, but neither of the sisters ever shifted."

Emmi gave me an assuring smile. "That does happen sometimes, but unfortunately, it means that you'll probably never shift, either, Elizabeth. Since you haven't by now, I would think you're not going to."

"I know," I told her. "I'm OK with that." The idea of shifting into a beast terrified me, even if it meant I could fend for myself and stop putting his family in danger.

"That's not all," Orin added. "Her mother wasn't a full shifter."

"What else was she?" Anton's eyes remained on his son as if I weren't there.

"Banshee."

"What?" he snapped.

"And that's not all." Orin didn't let his father calm down before he added, "Davis isn't Elizabeth's father. Her father was an incubus."

"Jesus Christ, son." Anton rose from his seat and began pacing behind the sofa. His reaction had me more afraid of what I was than originally finding out had. "You sure know how to pick them."

Orin hopped to his feet. "Watch it," he warned. "You're my father, but she's my wife."

His dad raised his hands, as if to say he understood, so Orin slowly sat back down. The last thing I wanted was another fight between them. I'd witnessed that the day I'd met his parents and it was the day I'd learned what Orin was.

Emmi was watching me with a careful eye, as if she were trying to size me up or see into my soul. "Have any abilities manifested?"

I was about to say *no* but had to take that back. "In Boston," I told her, "a man bumped into me and I saw his death. Right before we all saw his death. It happened just like I'd seen it. And, though I don't think this is an ability of some kind, a man came into our hotel room."

"A Balodis," Orin clarified.

"I felt an energy unlike anything I'd felt before and I was able to get away."

"She explained it as if all of his energy had left him and he just fell over." He glanced from me to his mom. "And then on the way here, she was asleep but sprung awake and knew someone was after us before we did."

"Was it a wolf?" Anton asked. After Orin nodded, he said, "She sensed a wolf before you and your brother?" Though I wondered why he left Karina out of it.

"Well." His mother slapped her hands against her thighs. "Looks like we have some research to do."

"What do you mean?" I asked.

"We need to find out where this is all coming from." She stood and crossed the room then ran her fingers over some book bindings. "We have all of the history here. I'm sure we'll figure this out."

"History?" I asked Orin quietly.

"We have books of our history. Like a grimoire of sorts."

I didn't know what that was, but I'd ask later. Whatever it was, hopefully Emmi would be able to help me.

"Are you coming?" Anton asked. At first, I was

confused, but then it was clear that he was talking to Orin.

"I'll stay here," Orin answered.

I leaned in and whispered, "Go where?"

"We're going for a run," Anton told me instead of letting Orin answer. "It would be a good time for Orin to be with his brothers."

"Why aren't you going?"

Orin looked into my eyes and I knew the answer. Because of me.

I hopped up off the sofa. "No way. You're not staying here because of me."

He stood and reached out for me, but I stepped away.

"No, Orin. If you'd normally go with your brothers, go. I'm fine here."

"Elizabeth."

"Orin." I folded my arms under my breasts so he'd know I wasn't budging on this and raised an eyebrow. His mother snorted behind me.

"I knew I liked this girl," she said with all the humor in her voice.

Orin sighed then pinched the bridge of his nose. "Fine. I'll go."

He hadn't been for a run in a while and he needed this. His runs did something for him that I didn't understand and couldn't replicate. He needed it and I wanted him to have it.

"I'll be here with her," Emmi assured him. "Are the women going as well?"

Anton shook his head. "They'll go on their own. My sons need some alone bonding time."

Orin pushed his fingers into my hair, his palms resting against my cheeks so that he could hold me there when his lips met mine.

"I won't be long," he whispered.

"Take as long as you need."

Once the men were gone, Emmi put both her hands on my shoulders. She was strong like the men. Tall, too, so she had to squat to look me in the eye.

"I'm going to help you," she assured me. "I'm going to help you figure out what you can do and how to control it. I grew up in a much more diverse pack. We'll figure this out." Then she hugged me and it was like being wrapped in a warm, soft blanket.

Once she'd let me go, I asked, "Why don't you hate me like the others do?"

"Diana doesn't hate you."

I sighed. "Fine. Blame me, then. You don't seem to."

Her eyes saddened as she took my hand in hers. "It's not your fault. Phillip did what any of them would do and I'm proud of him for protecting his brother's wife. Diana will come around."

"And Nell? She hated me when she thought I was human. What happens when she finds out..." I waved my hands around us. "All of this."

"They will all come around. Until then, you have Karina and you have me. You also have Orin. Because of that, his brothers will protect you."

"What if I don't want them to?"

Her eyes narrowed and her jaw set. "You don't have a choice in that. They'll do it because Orin wants it. None of them would let something happen to you because it would destroy him." A moment passed between us. "Now." She clapped her hands together. "You look like you could use a hot bath."

In that moment, nothing else sounded better.

Oddly, this place I'd never been to felt like home. At least for now, we could relax a little and not worry that someone was out to get me.

Unless it was Diana. I wasn't as sure that she'd leave me alone, but I'd trust Emmi.

And hope someone else would be there to stop her if I was wrong to.

Chapter Eleven

"From what I know, you're exhibiting abilities of both the banshee and the incubus," Emmi said as soon as we were alone together. This room was packed full of books. How she'd pulled the right one from the stack, I'd never know.

"But what does that even mean?" I asked. "I don't *feel* stronger. I still feel very weak compared to all of you."

She gave me that motherly look that said *my poor baby*. "Elizabeth, you're not weak. You're just... human." Then she chuckled loudly. "Well, I guess you're not even human. You have no human blood inside of you. But lineage is a weird thing."

"Can we start with what this even means?

Banshee? Incubus? I'd never heard of these things before."

Closing the book, she came toward me then motioned to the sofa. "Let's have a sit down." I followed because if it meant figuring out what I really was and what all of this meant, I'd follow this woman off a cliff if necessary. "A banshee is an Irish legend to the humans. Of course, we both know that they are very real. They're described as a spirit or fairy—usually female. They also typically have a wail—what they call a keen—that is the warning of impending death. Not all wail, though. But all do sense a coming death. They say that the sound of the wailing can be heard by those who are about to die or have recently died."

I furrowed my brows and ran my now-sweaty palms down my trousers. "Recently died?" She nodded. "I don't know that I have a wail." Then the memory of Phillip in the forest slammed into me like a tree falling from the heavens. "Do you think Phillip heard me crying in the forest?"

"If you were human, I would've said *no*, but now... maybe he did." I had more questions but didn't want to hurt her by talking about her dead son. "But the banshee acts as a guardian or messenger of death. From what you told me about the vision you had, it seems to fit."

"Does that mean I'm going to see more deaths?"

"Most likely." She put her strong hand on my much smaller one. "But we're going to work on it so that you can shield yourself. Seeing death after death would take its toll and we don't want that."

Nervous butterflies let loose in my stomach at what I wanted to tell her. Orin had told me that they were an open family, but it wasn't something I'd participated in yet. "After it happened... I didn't want Orin to touch me." My eyes filled with tears. "I can't see him die once let alone twice."

"Oh, sweetheart." She pulled me into her arms. "Of course you wouldn't want that. We're going to work on a shield. A way for you to protect yourself, but it could also come in handy."

"Audrey said that too." Those tears streaked down my cheeks, landing on her shirt.

"If there's a coming fight, which we all know is going to happen, you might want to assure yourself that everyone is going to come back and if you have a vision, the boys would be able to plan around it to stop it from happening. Your visions aren't just for you to see that someone is going to die. You can also use it to protect those you love."

"That's what Orin said," I told her, blowing out a slow breath. "I didn't believe him because I thought he just wanted to be able to touch me."

Her chest jiggled with laughter. "I'm sure that was part of it. I know my boys very well."

At least it brought some levity to the situation.

"Now." She sat me back up so that I could dry my eyes and we could keep talking. "The enhanced senses that you experienced on your way here as well as the energy draining—"

"Energy draining?"

"From what you described, that's what it sounds like happened in your hotel room. Those are both powers of the incubus. Very rare powers and very useful. You say you're weak, but if you can drain the energy of an attacker? You should feel very powerful."

For the first time since all of this had started, a small spark of hope sprung inside of me. Orin had made it clear early on that he'd die to protect me, but if I could help protect myself, then he shouldn't have to.

"So what is an incubus?"

Emmi flipped the book open to show me a drawing of a very handsome man. "It's a male demon, some say spirit, but it's always in the form of a very attractive man. His main deed is that he likes to visit sleeping women and engage in sexual activity."

My spine snapped straight. "My aunt said that my mother was very much in love with my father... My real father. That the charm didn't work on her."

"That may very well have been the case. Just because that is what most do doesn't mean that's what all do. Nothing is black or white. There is a lot of gray area in everything."

"So, I'm an incubus? But you said they are male."

"You can't be an incubus because those are male. A female incubus would be a succubus. Same idea, though. A succubus would seduce men in their sleep."

My eyes widened and my face heated to the point that I would've bet it looked like the surface of the sun. "I didn't seduce Orin in his sleep. He came to me at a ball my father held."

She chuckled again, as if what I'd just said was the most ridiculous thing she'd ever heard. "Oh, honey. I believe those powers only work on human men. Your powers of seduction work for a very different reason when it comes to my son."

I slapped a hand over my face. How embarrassing.

"So." She snapped the book closed again and set it on the table. "We're going to work on all of this tomorrow, but what I want you to practice is envisioning a shield going around you. It's going to be a mental shield, of course, but I want you to see it in your mind. That's how you're going to be able to protect yourself so that every person you bump into isn't invited in. You won't see if they are about to die unless you want to. Though, to be honest, you won't see many either way. Most people aren't on the verge of death on a given day. But doing this will at least make you feel more in control of your life."

"Thank you so much, Emmi." I reached out to hug her. She accepted my affection willingly, which wasn't something I'd expected the first time I'd met her. His parents had been angry that he'd married a human without even consulting them. It had been too late when they'd shown up.

He'd already ruined me for anyone else.

We were still talking when the men loudly entered the house again. They were laughing and from what I could tell, everything was good between them. At some point, they split up because only Orin and Anton entered the study, both with windblown hair, wearing loose pants and disheveled shirts and no shoes.

Orin came over to me and kissed the top of my head before lifting my chin so he could get a really good look at me. "What's going on?" He glanced at his mother with the question all over her face. "You look like you've been crying."

"I was," I told him. No sense trying to hide it.

"What did you do?" he demanded, taking a step toward his mother.

Emmi slowly stood, almost eye to eye with Orin, but his father slid in between them. "You may be younger than me, son, but I've got the experience. Don't talk to your mother that way."

"Orin." I put myself in front of him and placed my hands on his chest. "She didn't do anything except help me figure out what I am. I cried because the thought of seeing your death over and over hurts me to my very core. That's all."

"I've told you, son," Emmi said gently. "This is your mate. That means she has the protection of every person in this pack. I'd never do anything to hurt her or let anything happen to her. I've sworn that."

Orin's shoulders relaxed and he wrapped his arms around me and pulled me to his chest. "I'm sorry."

"I understand. When it comes to your mate, you'll do anything."

"Come on." He pulled me behind him out of the room, up the stairs, and didn't stop until we were inside his room. Our room for the amount of time we were staying here. "You're really all right?"

"Yes." I tried giving him my best smile, though I couldn't imagine what it looked like. "I really am. Your mother was wonderful. She explained everything." I gazed up at him through my eyelashes. "Even explained that I can't be an incubus, but I'd be a succubus. Apparently, I have the power to seduce men."

A new kind of fire lit in his eyes and he grabbed my hips with his big hands. "You're damn right you do."

The first button on his shirt popped open easily. "I have no idea what I'm doing most of the time. I only know what you've taught me."

He thrust his fingers into my hair and caressed my cheek with the palm of his hand as I continued working on his shirt. Once I'd worked all the buttons, I pushed the fabric off his shoulders. He made much quicker work of my top and brassiere and suddenly, I was standing in front of him, breasts bare to him and the air.

First, he brought his mouth to mine, holding my head in place with one hand and wrapping the other around my waist. His mouth was warm and wet, coaxing me to part my lips so that he could sneak his tongue into my mouth. I'd never even heard about this kind of kiss before marrying Orin and now... I could melt into him.

My breasts pressed against his chest, his natural warmth scurrying over my skin. It was like he was the fire and I was desperate for heat. Working a little room between us, his tongue stroked mine as the hand that had been around my waist trailed down my chest, between my breasts, then down my stomach. Suddenly, he moved the other to the same spot and that was when I realized he was undoing my trousers.

Orin trailed his lips across my cheek and down my neck, pushing the trousers and my underthings down my legs before cupping one of my breasts. When his lips wrapped around one of my nipples, my muscles clenched. Everything he did, every way he touched me, had me wanting him more and more.

"This has nothing to do with what you are," he

murmured against my breast. "This is just you." He took one of my hands from his shoulder and brought it down to his pants-covered cock. It was hard and thick and straining against the material. "You do this to me, Elizabeth." He helped me there then used his index finger of his other hand to raise my chin. "You do. Because you're beautiful and I've never wanted anyone like I want you. Not because you're part succubus. I'd want you if you were human. I did want you when you were human."

Orin accepted me the way no one else ever had. He was happy with me, however—or whatever—I was. It was a safety that I'd never felt in my life.

"I know." I kissed the top of his nose. "And I know what you like." My heart sped up. I'd only done this a couple of times, but I knew how much he liked it, so I was determined to get good at it.

After wiggling my hand out from under his, I undid his trousers as quickly as I could and pushed them down. After all, he already had me completely naked and I wanted him to be too. Then I slowly lowered myself to my knees. He growled in his chest, but this one was different. It wasn't a warning, it wasn't anger... it was full of pleasure.

First, I wrapped my small hand around his cock and stroked it twice like he'd shown me. Of course, I had nothing to compare Orin to, but he was long and thick to me. Even more so when the moon was full. Then I wet my lips and wrapped them around him. He groaned and let his head fall back to hit the door with a *thud*.

"Fuck, Elizabeth."

When he said those words, the words you weren't supposed to say in polite company, it pushed me further and made me want to do more. I wanted to be the one to make him say it again.

He'd shown me how to do this. How to take him in my mouth and move my head and stroke him with my tongue. I did all of that but let myself loose. When he hit the back of my throat, a gagging noise came from within and then I pulled him out and licked from the bottom to the tip.

"That's it." He yanked me off the floor and carried me to the bed, letting me down with a bounce.

"I wasn't done," I whined. He'd never once let me do that until he had his orgasm and that was something I wanted to try.

"Yes. You are." He pinned my hands to the bed and let his body barely brush mine as he kissed me deeply, his tongue reaching further and him stealing my very breath. Then he was back on his feet, pulling me to the edge of the bed.

These things... oral sex... I'd never known they existed. Probably in my father's society, they didn't. But they were missing out.

Orin wasted no time licking me and pushing my thighs apart. Mostly, he liked to take his time with me, but today... wasn't the day for that. He licked me and pushed two fingers inside me. It was aggressive, but aggressive in pleasure. My back arched off the bed, my stomach clenched, and I was at the peak in almost no time. My orgasm slammed into me and something so violent shouldn't have felt so good.

Once my muscles relaxed, Orin was over me, pushing inside of me. He stretched me almost to the max. That was reserved for the full moon. At that time, any larger and it would've been painful. Orin slammed into me again and again, pushing me against the mattress. This was something that should've hurt, or I would've thought hurt, but it didn't. If anything, I wanted more. I wanted him to go harder and faster and soon, I was back at the peak, with him tumbling after me.

His head dropped to my shoulder as we both clung to each other, fighting for the very air.

"Damn, Elizabeth." He slowly pulled out of me and kissed me at the same languid pace.

"Damn Elizabeth?" I asked. "I didn't even do anything."

He chuckled, his body vibrating against mine. "Sure, you didn't."

But I had to smile. His reaction and his words were all I needed to know that I made him feel as good as he made me.

"Do you want to clean up or stay just like this?" he asked as he rested his head on my shoulder.

"Stay like this." I giggled as he let more of his body weight press me into the mattress. "But I should clean up."

Then he was off me and I sat up. It wasn't until I was halfway to the bathroom attached to his bedroom that something occurred to me and I stopped in my tracks before turning to him. "They all could hear us, couldn't they?"

Orin turned toward me and wet his lips. "Yes. They could hear us if they wanted to, but I told you before, we actively try not to hear what any of us are doing in the bedroom. Could you imagine the trauma of our childhood if we didn't?"

I slapped a hand over my face and turned to head back to the bathroom.

He really hadn't needed to say that.

At least there was one thing for certain. Even if any of them had heard us, I wouldn't be judged as a whore for enjoying sex with my husband.

In my other life, I may have been burned at the stake as a witch for that very thing.

Chapter Twelve

That night might've been the most restful sleep I'd gotten since Phillip had died in the woods. He hadn't haunted my dreams that night and being here with Orin's family gave me a sense of safety that I hadn't felt in a while.

I was always safe with Orin. This was like extra, extra protection.

Whatever it was, I woke up rested and ready to work with his mother on controlling my new abilities.

"Touch me again," Emmi said, to which I sighed. I'd been making contact with her all morning and nothing had happened.

"Have you thought that maybe you're just not

close to death?" Karina offered. She'd been with us all morning.

Emmi chuckled. "That is the hope, isn't it?" She put her hands on her hips and watched me with contemplation. "I'm not sure what else to do. How do we find someone we know is close to death to see if she can control it or block it?"

I cringed. That was the last thing I wanted to do.

"Why don't we work on the energy draining," Karina offered. She'd pulled her dark-blonde hair back into a braid to work with me today.

"Uh, no," I told her. "I'm not doing that to my mother-in-law."

Emmi snorted. "I'm stronger than I look."

Which was actually terrifying because Emmi was the strongest, sturdiest-looking woman I'd ever seen. Her shoulders were broad—not quite as broad as her son's. She was tall. Her legs were thick with muscle. I had no doubt she could handle anything that was thrown at her.

But the man at the hotel had also been strong and he'd gone down hard.

"How did you do it at the hotel?" Karina asked. "Don't worry. You don't have to practice on your mother-in-law. You can use me."

My eyes widened. "You think I want to do that, either?"

She shrugged. "We could get Diana in here."

Emmi scowled. "Stop with that. She's mourning and unfortunately, her anger has unfairly landed on Elizabeth."

"I don't think it's unfair," I said under my breath.

"What was that?" Karina waited with eyebrows raised. She'd heard it. Of course she'd heard it. She had wolf ears.

I just shook my head and let it go. Both of those women would tell me—again—that Phillips' death wasn't my fault. They'd be wrong. He wouldn't have been in those woods protecting me if I would've stayed home and not insisted on being "helpful."

"All right." Karina scoffed. "Why don't we work on the enhanced hearing? That could be very helpful and won't hurt anyone." She grabbed my wrists and led me to the sofa then gently pushed me so that I'd sit down. "The men are all outside. What are they doing?" When I just kept my eyes on her, she shook her head. "Focus. You were asleep in the car, which meant you weren't mentally in your own way and you did hear what was out there long before the rest of us did."

"It was a couple of seconds," I countered.

"That's a lot when you're talking about our hearing," Emmi assured me while patting my shoulder.

"Now," Karina began. "Close your eyes and take deep breaths. Concentrate. Maybe focus on Orin since you have a deep connection with him. If what I heard coming from your room last night says anything, it's that your connection is very deep."

My eyes flew open and my mouth dropped open with disbelief that she'd just said that at all, but especially in front of his mother.

"Calm down. I only heard a second because I'd accidentally dropped my guard. It's fine."

I let the burning sensation prickle at my skin because there was nothing I could say that would make me more comfortable with this situation. So I did what she'd instructed. I closed my eyes and focused.

At first, nothing happened. Then I started thinking about last night. The way Orin's fingers had trailed along my skin. The way his mouth had felt when he'd taken a nipple into it. And then...

I heard it. The pounding of something. A hammer? Yes. A hammer against metal. A nail? They were fixing something out behind the house. The direction echoed in my brain, but I was sure. It was coming from the back of the house.

"Are they building something in the back yard?"

Emmi put her hands on her hips, looming over me like a severe school marm. "I don't know, Elizabeth. Are they?"

I swallowed hard. "Orin's using a hammer to pound in a nail. That's what I'm hearing. Are they building something?"

Karina grabbed my hand and pulled me up before dragging me through the house to the door that opened on the back. Once we were out in the sunshine, it all began to make sense.

Orin was, in fact, pounding some nails with a hammer. All of the men were dressed in a way that I hadn't seen before, outside of magazines that showed cowboys in the West. They were wearing jeans and button-down white shirts. All working hard at whatever job they were doing.

"What are they building?" I asked quietly, unable to take my eyes off my husband. His muscles strained at he swung the hammer again—the nail went in with one hit.

"A new shed. We need some storage space and also somewhere out of the rain for them to put their clothes before they shift."

Karina released a pleasant sigh. "It's very easy to watch, isn't it?"

Emmi *tsked* and shook her head. These were her sons here. "So you can definitely hear things far away. Keep practicing and soon you won't have to focus so much. Come on."

The three of us were back inside—the kitchen this time—after deciding to make the men some sandwiches. I wasn't sure where Aras and Diana were, but it didn't surprise me that they weren't here with us. It seemed that they made it a point to be wherever I wasn't. And that was fine. Seeing baby Ruby filled me with so much guilt since I considered it my fault that she was going to grow up without a father.

We were halfway through making the men lunch when something crashed outside. Emmi ran to the window, then her eyes widened. "Karina, come with me. Elizabeth, stay here. No matter what happens, stay here."

They hurried out, but that left me not knowing what was going on. I took Emmi's place at the window.

The Vilkatas family were shifting. Clothes were ripping off their bodies as they turned into the animals I still wasn't accustomed to seeing. They didn't turn into wolves like the animals that roamed the Earth. They were more like wolfmen.

Standing on two legs, running on all fours. Long snout, hairy.

This was a fight, but with whom?

My fingers gripped the edge of the sink. That was my family out there and I was putting them in danger. The last thing I could handle was one of them being hurt because of me again.

And which one was Orin?

I hadn't seen his brothers shift before. Just his dad when they'd gotten into the fight over me and I was now realizing they all looked alike with subtle differences.

So which one was Orin?

Two more wolves came from the side of the house. That had to be Emmi and Karina, so I made mental notes of their differences.

Karina wasn't as tall as Emmi and her coat had a reddish tint. Emmi's had some white in it, as did her fur.

Contemplating going out there was a bad idea. That would only get people more hurt.

"I can't believe they left you alone." A man's voice came from behind me. I'd been so focused on the fight happening outside that I'd forgotten to be on alert—to focus my senses. "Idiots."

Damn it.

After swallowing hard and summoning all of the courage I had inside me, I turned to face the man who'd gotten inside the house.

I didn't recognize the man from the house they'd kept me in, but that wouldn't have been shocking. He could have been a Balodis. I didn't know them all. He was tall—of course—his hair long enough to be held back in a ponytail, and he had a large scar running down the side of his face, making everything about him more menacing.

"What do you want?" I asked, pushing myself hard back into the edge of the countertop. Any space I could put between the two of us, the better.

He cocked his head to the side as a slow grin raised his cheeks. "Revenge."

I furrowed my brows. The Balodis had never wanted me out of revenge. They'd wanted my blood to help recreate their line.

"Revenge? For what?"

He slid across the floor until he was able to box me in with his arms and large body. I willed my heart to calm down. Panicking wasn't going to help me.

"You ask a lot of questions." He sneered.

"I asked two."

An animal growl made me push back further, the

countertop digging into my back. Wait. I had things that I could use. Last time I'd used my energy draining, I'd been scared. I was scared now. This could work.

Quickly, I grabbed his arms with my hands and tried everything Emmi had told me to do. I focused. I wanted his life force... Nothing happened. When I relaxed my hands, a vision hit.

The man was over me as he was right now. A wolf launched itself at him, taking him to the ground. Those thick talons sliced through the man's neck, spilling blood everywhere.

I yanked my hands away from him like his skin was fire. The problem was I didn't know how long it'd be before this vision happened.

Then a wolf launched itself at the man, taking him to the ground. The loud echo of growls filled the air and I slapped my hands over my ears to keep it out. Enhanced senses weren't needed to hear this fight and I wanted to close my eyes to keep it out but couldn't stop watching even though I knew how this would end.

The talons slashed the man's neck, spilling blood all over the floor. Exactly how I'd seen it.

The good news was my power worked and Emmi wasn't close to death. The bad news was I'd seen that twice and my stomach turned at the very real blood flooding the kitchen.

The wolf turned to me, then shifted back into Orin. "I should've killed that guy a long time ago."

It wasn't until I saw that it was him that I started to vibrate. My hands were shaking so badly that I couldn't push away the strands of hair hanging over my face.

"Hey." Orin slid in front of me in all of his naked glory. "It's OK. You're OK."

"They're never going to stop, are they?" Even my voice was shaking. The boldness and strength I'd had when the man had appeared had completely disappeared.

"What?" He furrowed his brows. "This wasn't about you, Elizabeth. This wasn't the Balodis pack."

Finally, I lifted my eyes to look at him. "What?"

"This was—"

"Jesus," Ivan bellowed, and suddenly, the entire pack was in the kitchen with us. "Put on some clothes."

Roman tossed Orin a pair of pants that had come from who-knows-where. Orin quickly put them on, though he didn't seem to care that he'd been standing naked in front of everyone. And I did mean *everyone* except Diana and Aras. They'd disappeared earlier and I didn't know where they were.

"This wasn't about me?" I asked him quietly.

Daniel snorted. "Kind of crazy that not every-thing revolves around you, huh?" Orin growled and Daniel held up his hands to say he was done.

"No," Orin told me, but he continued to glare at his brothers. "This wasn't about you. This was about us. They probably thought they could take us by surprise because you're here. That we'd be preoccupied."

"How did they know she's here, though?" Roman asked. No one had an answer.

Emmi sighed. "I guess we have some cleanup to do." She was looking at the man dead on her floor. I pushed myself further against Orin's side because that was where I felt the safest. His warmth was everything.

"I didn't have a choice," he told her.

She waved him off. "Of course you didn't. I just wish it had been outside." She pointed at Daniel and Ivan. "You two, take care of the body. We'll get the cleaner." Karina followed her out of the room as Daniel and Ivan worked on getting the man out of the house.

As they lifted him, more blood spilled from his

body to the floor creating a grotesque puddle. It'd be a miracle if Emmi was able to get it all out.

Only Anton, Roman, Orin, and I remained.

"I can help them." Though the thought of it turned my stomach.

"No." Orin squeezed my shoulders. "You need to stay with me."

"You can't stay here," Anton said gently. Orin didn't react. "It's too dangerous. If the other packs know she's here now, they'll think it's a great time to attack. Like today. That we'll be so focused on protecting her we won't be ready for multiple packs." Then he looked directly at me. "This wasn't about you. This was about a long-standing struggle for power." He sighed. "It was just bad timing that you are here for it."

"Where would they go?" Roman asked his father.

"Emmi and I think Elizabeth should search out her real father."

My eyes widened. Meeting that man had never crossed my mind as a serious option. "What?"

"I think it's the best way," Anton told me. "He's an incubus. That means he runs with demons. He'd be able to protect you better than anyone."

Orin scoffed, but his father held up a hand.

"No one would look for her," Anton said.

That, Orin couldn't argue with.

"Did your aunt or your mother's letter lead you to believe he'd meet you?" Roman asked.

There wasn't much about him in the letters that was current. "No, but I from everything I've read and was told, he didn't turn his back on my mother because he didn't love her. They thought it was safer that way. He loved her enough to let her go, knowing that she was carrying me." I looked up at my husband. "That has to mean he wanted to protect me, right?"

"Right." He wet his lips quickly then turned back to his brother and father. "We'll leave tonight. But we'll go back to Boston first. See if Audrey has any idea where we should start looking that she didn't write out."

"Won't going back put her in more danger?" Bringing danger to people who meant something to me wasn't what I wanted to do. Audrey had a special place in my heart because she was my mother's sister. I wouldn't exactly call it love but it was a connection. One I'd never had.

"It could," Anton said gently. "But it's a chance you're going to have to take."

"Everything on her list is old. It's the things

about my mother's relationship with him. Not where to find him now."

Anton shook his head. "Go in the morning. After all of this"—he waved his hand around to indicate the fight outside—"it'd be better to be well-rested."

One more night here and then I was going to try to find my real father.

Chapter Thirteen

GETTING BACK to Boston took less time than leaving it. I didn't know why and honestly, I didn't care. Karina and Roman didn't come with us this time. It was decided that they were more needed at home, given the attack that had just happened and the fact that the Vilkatas were down three wolves.

Phillip because he was dead.

Diana because she was mourning, though Karina told me that she wouldn't be able to use that much longer. Everyone was expected to pull their own weight and if Diana remained with the pack, she'd have to participate. Though that could mean taking care of any of the children while everyone else went out to fight.

No one wanted Ruby to be an orphan and Daniel Jr. still needed to be taken care of.

Aras wasn't allowed to fight because she was pregnant. Pregnancies were taken very seriously since that was the way they grew the pack. Not all shifters were affected by the whole *dying in childbirth* thing dropping their birth rate.

We were in Boston standing outside my aunt's house before lunch. When we'd left, I thought that was the last time I'd see her, which had created a weird, bittersweet emotion inside of me. I took a deep breath and climbed the steps then knocked on her door.

Her face widened in surprise when she opened it. "Elizabeth? What happened? Why are you back?"

After swallowing my nerves down, I said, "I have to find my father."

She closed her eyes for several seconds then sighed and stepped back. "You might as well come in."

Orin followed me into the house and sat beside me on the same sofa I'd sat on when I'd first met her.

"Remember, Elizabeth. Finding your father isn't a good idea." Audrey sat on the edge of the chair kitty-corner from the couch. "What happened?"

After telling her everything that had happened, I

added, "The Vilkatas think that the best way to protect me right now is to find my father." I swallowed hard. "To me it seems like if she would've stayed, he would have loved me. Wanted to protect me."

"That's true," she agreed. "But your mother left for a reason. Leaving was the way to protect you."

"Why?"

Audrey sighed. "Telling you this is going against a promise I made a long time ago. Something I don't do lightly." She swallowed hard. "Your father was worried that if his people discovered you, they would kill you simply because he'd procreated with a wolf. Neither of them thought our pack would ever discover you. Without shifting, they can't find you."

"He did." I pointed at Orin. He said that the pull of his mate string had led to me. While I wasn't entirely sure what that meant, it meant something.

"That's different. The mate bond is something else." She leaned forward to take my hands into hers. "Elizabeth, I worry that they'll kill you now before ever hearing you out."

A menacing growl came from beside me. "I won't let that happen. Tell us how to find him," Orin told her, stepping into the conversation for the first time.

Audrey sighed again. "The Balodis packhouse is

not far from your house. Maybe six hours by car." She stood and went over to the desk in the corner to begin rummaging through the papers. "Thora met him in town, which means their home base can't be far." She came back and laid a map on the table in front of us. "The Balodis packhouse is here." She pointed to one spot on the map. "From what Thora said, I imagine the incubus came from here." She circled another point on the map. "But I think if you just go to town, you'll find at least one and can follow them back."

"Thank you," I told her with all sincerity. Without her help, who knew what we'd be doing?

"Then it's time for us to catch a train." Orin gently pulled me to my feet. We'd drive the "borrowed" car back to Boston and now we'd leave it there.

We were going home just to leave again.

Orin took care of everything. He got our tickets, left the car—telling me that Roman would come to get it to return it—and got us settled on the train. It would be torture waiting all the hours to get back home and leave again.

The prospect of meeting my real father—one who presumably loved me—had anxious energy making me feel on edge. I twisted my fingers together again and again. Finally, Orin put his hand over mine so I'd stop.

"You don't have to worry, Elizabeth. You know I'm going to take care of you."

"I know." Because I couldn't fiddle with my fingers, I nervously nibbled on my bottom lip.

"Tell me about your training with my mother," he said, turning to me. "Is it working?"

"I don't know. I mean, yes. I've learned how to broaden my senses some. It doesn't always work."

While cupping my cheek, he ran a thumb down my cheekbone. "That will come with practice."

"I know. Blocking seeing people's deaths? I don't think that works at all. I saw the man in the kitchen's death. I couldn't stop it. But I do feel better that it's only imminent death because I won't see it with every person I touch all day long."

He cocked his head to the side and grinned. "Are you touching many people throughout the day?"

My cheeks burned. "Of course not, but people do bump into me. I know I should want to prevent any deaths that I can but it's incredibly hard to keep seeing it."

"I know it is," he said quietly. "Try it. Here." He waved his hand around. "See what you find out."

I was going to protest, but we were here for a

while, so what better chance? However, the only way to know if I was controlling it or not was to see who actually died. Either way, I decided to do it so that I could have the reminder that I wasn't going to see it from every person I touched.

Hesitantly, I pushed up from my seat. The train was moving, so I was careful. Most people, I just trailed my fingers over their arm and they didn't even notice. Then a woman bumped into me and it came.

She was pale and kind of green. She sat down in her seat and closed her eyes. Her breath came rapidly and then... stopped. The little girl beside her shakes the woman and then begins to cry and yell for help.

There was nothing I could do to help this woman and at least her death wouldn't be violent.

I turned away and run right into another woman. She was young, beautiful. Probably had a lot to live for. But the vision slammed into me, anyway.

She stepped off the train at our next stop. Her heel caught and she tripped, sliding into the opening between the train and the platform. Only a few saw it happen and called for help, but the train began to move, pulling her under. Her death was very violent.

I gasped and the woman asked, "Are you all right?"

"I'm... I'm fine," I tell her because what was I

supposed to say? *Don't get off the train.* She'll think I'm psychotic.

She keeps walking, but I hurry back to Orin. I saw imminent deaths. So this would be happening soon. There was nothing any of us could do to save the first woman. Maybe there was something to save the second.

"Orin," I gasp, out of breath from hurrying back to him.

"What did you see?" He pulled me down next to him. After laying it all out for him, he glanced around looking for the woman. "Her?" His head nodded toward her.

"Yes," I whispered.

"I'll make sure it doesn't happen."

The train had slowed and was grinding to a stop, with both of us watching the woman. When she got up, Orin slipped in behind her. There weren't too many people leaving our car, which was probably why not many saw her fall in my vision. When they got the door near us, I could just see her trip. Orin's strong hand reacted, grabbing her arm to keep her from falling.

"Thank you so much," she said, sounding as out of breath as I had when I'd told Orin the story. "I'm so clumsy."

"It's not a problem. I'm glad you weren't hurt."

She smiled up at him with a wide grin and sparkling, green eyes. I sat back so I couldn't see anymore. Hearing was bad enough.

"Are you getting off here?" she asked. "I feel like I owe you a coffee."

My stomach tightened. Of course she'd want to spend time with Orin. He was beautiful and sexy and powerful. I wouldn't be the only person to think that.

"No, thank you," he told me. "My wife and I are continuing our trip."

The woman's face fell but she recovered quickly, gave him a curt nod then continued on her way.

Once he was back beside me, the adrenaline running through me stopped and now, I began to vibrate and this was where all the emotions of what I'd seen would hit me.

"Elizabeth?" he asked with concern. "Are you all right? I saved her, sweetheart. She's all right."

"I know." That voice didn't sound like mine. "I need... I don't know." Then I did. Without knowing *how* he'd make it happen, if I said the words, he would make it happen. "Make me feel better."

His brows furrowed and then he realized what I meant. "Come with me." He took my hand and led me to the back of the train car, where the restroom was. We'd had an overnight car on the way here but there weren't any available this time. After nudging me inside, he followed and then shut the door, hitting the lock so that no one would be able to get inside.

Once we were secure inside, Orin's mouth met mine. It was aggressive and demanding. Everything I needed it to be. His hands worked at a furious pace, pushing my shirt up my thighs until he could pull my underwear down.

Everything I'd seen washed away and all I could focus on was him... his movements... the way he touched me. His hard cock pressed against the inside of my thigh. This might be quick, but it was exactly what I needed.

His warmth rushed over me. He kissed down my neck to as close to my breasts as he could get. We weren't going to be able to undress, but for this... we didn't need to.

Orin spun me around, my hands bracing against the wall. With very little room to maneuver, he made it look easy. With the skirt of my dress up over my behind, Orin pushed inside me. I'd been so focused on his touches that I hadn't realized he'd undone his trousers.

I sighed and my forehead hit the wall quietly, but his hand snaked up the front of me to my neck and pulled me back as he moved inside of me. This right here was exactly what I needed. He turned my head almost too far so that he could kiss me, his tongue sneaking into my mouth—he braced my weight with an arm around my waist. I didn't have to do anything but enjoy the ride.

He'd barely caressed my clitoris before I was coming undone. The sounds coming from my mouth were too loud and I couldn't control them. Orin wrapped his hand over my mouth to muffle my orgasm and once I'd quieted down, he let out a low groan and stopped moving.

"Was that what you needed?" he whispered in my ear. I nodded my response because I wouldn't be able to form words right now.

Gently, he pulled out of me. The water turned on then something cool touched my most sensitive area. He was taking care of me. I'd have to go back out into the train, where everyone else was, and he didn't want me doing that with his... seed running down my legs. Then he helped put me back together.

"You go back to our seats," he told me. "I'll follow you in a minute."

Again, I nodded, but then I used both hands on

his cheeks to pull him down for another kiss before slipping out of the restroom.

If there was one thing that was certain in my life, among all of the uncertainty, it was that Orin would never deny me anything that I wanted or needed.

Even if it was in the restroom of a very public train car.

My father—Henry Davis—would have been appalled to see what I'd become.

I was in my seat maybe two minutes when Orin dropped into his.

"Thank you." I kissed his cheek. "I feel much better."

The corners of his mouth turned up before he said, "It's not a hardship for me, Elizabeth. Though I can't say I wasn't surprised, due to where we are."

I glanced around quickly, but no one seemed to be paying any attention to us. "Do you think they heard me?"

He shook his head. "I think I quieted you down well enough. Listen." He arranged himself so that he was facing me and took both of my hands into his. "I understand that you're working through what you see. I'm happy to be the one you work that out on. But we can also talk about it whenever you're ready to."

Tears burned my eyes. He was right. Every time I saw a death—except the one in his kitchen—I needed him inside of me. Was it the healthiest way to deal with it? I liked to think so.

"I know," I whispered. Any louder and those tears would've started to fall.

I spent the rest of the train ride with my arms wrapped around Orin's arm and my head on his shoulder, enjoying the fact that with him right now, I was safe and could pretend that all of the other stuff didn't exist.

When the train jerked to a stop, my eyes flew open. I hadn't intended to fall asleep, but I must've and it hadn't been for long. We weren't at the stop we would need to go home. No, this was the stop needed to find my real father.

"Are you ready?" Orin asked.

Not at all. But still, I said, "Yes."

Orin helped me off the train and then gave our baggage ticket to the man who worked for the railroad. Now, we had to wait.

He wrapped his arm around my waist and pulled me close. His lips pressed against my head, then he whispered, "There's a man to your right who's been watching you since we got off the train." Surprised, I started to turn my head. "Don't look now. It will be too obvious. I'll handle this."

Looking up at him, I asked, "What're you going to do?"

"Rip his throat out."

"Orin." I placed a hand on his chest to calm him down. "He's just looking at me, right? He might be human."

"He's not." Orin glanced back over and I wished with everything I had that I could look over. I would. I just had to make it look natural. "That's it." Orin moved in that direction and I grabbed his hand at the last moment to either stop him or make him take me with him.

This gave me the chance to see whom he was talking about. A tall man, thinner than Orin, with dark hair perfectly styled back away from his face, stood there watching me. His gray eyes met my blue ones and he took a deep breath, then began his way over to us.

Orin pushed me behind him. His way of saying he was here to protect me.

"Stop," he said with a growl. The man stopped but didn't look bothered by the growl. He simply put his hands in the pockets of his pants.

"You must be Elizabeth," he said, his eyes

directly on me, as if a huge wolf shifter weren't standing right in front of me.

"How do you know her?" Orin demanded, his skin vibrating with energy.

"She looks just like her mother." This was when he finally looked at Orin. "I'm Coltar Hilt. I'm Elizabeth's father."

My eyes widened as I stepped out from behind Orin. "How did you know we were here?"

"I'll tell you everything," he said. "But first, we have to leave here. There are too many watchful eyes." He took several steps closer, though Orin didn't relax an inch. "I have a place we can go. No one will find us there."

Orin's muscles tightened, but this was what we were here for. "Let's go, then."

Chapter Fourteen

"I have a car we can take." Coltar—my father—grabbed one of the bags that I hadn't noticed had been set beside us. Orin took the other bag and with his free hand, he grabbed mine.

"Where are we going?" Orin asked, the threat of death to anyone who dared try to harm me clear in his tone.

"I have a safehouse. Someplace no one knows about. We'll go there and I'll explain everything as far as I know."

"How did you know we were coming?" I asked when he stopped next to a Ford Model A. I didn't know much about car things usually but had seen one before and had asked Orin what it was.

"Audrey got a message to me," he said as he

opened the passenger side to grab some rope. There was a luggage rack on the back of the car. He put Orin's bag and then mine. We hadn't taken a lot with us to begin with, but we did need what we had. "It was a great cost to her and was dangerous so I knew this was important."

Orin pulled me away, far enough to where Coltar wouldn't be able to hear us.

"I'm going to sit in the front with him," he told me. "You get in the back. I want to be able to stop anything he might pull."

"You think he came to find me to hurt me?"

"I don't know. I don't trust him just yet. He's a demon."

I snapped my mouth closed too hard before saying, "So am I, right? Or a part of me?"

"It's not the same thing. He just said Audrey told him we were coming, but she told us she didn't know for sure where he was. How did she tell him? A telegram?"

I put my hands on his chest because that tended to have a calming effect on him. "These are great questions to ask him when we get to the... what'd he call it? Safehouse? I'll do whatever you tell me to Orin because I trust you the way I could never trust anyone else. And you know more about this world than I do. All worlds, actually. But this is my father and I want to find out about him."

"I know, baby. I want that for you. Just also let me protect you."

I pushed up onto my toes and kissed his cheek. "No argument from me."

We made our way back over to Coltar, who had our bags strapped down. "I'm not going to hurt her," he told my husband.

"Make sure that you don't." There was so much threat in those innocent words that someone who wasn't a demon might've gotten worried. Not him, though.

Once we were all in the car, with me in the back seat directly behind Orin and Coltar behind the wheel, Coltar said, "It's not far, actually. I've found that hiding in plain sight has its benefits." He glanced over his shoulder at me and then back onto the road. "It seems Thora had the same thoughts."

"Why do you say that?" I asked.

"Because she didn't run very far. Most people would try to get on the other side of the world away from whatever it was that had sent them running. Not her. She only ran hours away."

"Are you what she was running from?" Orin asked, the acid from my stomach burning my throat.

"In a way." But he didn't elaborate. "I'll let you two clean up and make some dinner. It won't be much. My wife is the cook in the family."

My stomach clenched. His wife. Audrey had told me he had a wife. And children. I had siblings.

The house he brought us to was modest in size and once inside, it was clear to me it hadn't been updated in years. There were a few modern amenities in the kitchen—like a refrigerator—but beyond that, it looked older.

Once Orin and I had cleaned ourselves up and changed our clothes, we came back downstairs to a delicious smell of chicken and potatoes. There was something garlic and... something else.

"This smells delicious," I told Coltar as I came into the kitchen with Orin right behind me. He was setting everything on the table in the kitchen. The table was a small square with four chairs around it, but we'd only be using three... I thought.

"It's one of the only things I can cook." Coltar put three glasses of water on the table.

"It's more than I can cook," I admitted.

"That's not true anymore." Orin pulled my chair out for me. I definitely noticed that he'd chosen the chair for me across the table from Coltar.

"That's true." The cooking classes I'd taken had

started to pay off. I could make a decent dinner now, but Orin was still the better cook. Coltar watched the two of us, a slight pinch to his brow telling me he didn't understand what we were talking about. "I've taken some cooking lessons from a widow in town. It's helped."

The three of us sat at the table and began to make our plates. Orin offered me the chicken first. I took a small amount, not sure that I'd even be able to eat that the way that my stomach was tumbling over itself.

"Your mother didn't teach you how to cook?" Coltar asked. "If memory serves, she was a fantastic cook."

He didn't know. He didn't know that my mother was dead or at least that she'd died in childbirth and never had the chance to teach me anything. Each morsel of information I received about my mother got tucked away into a special place only for her.

"She's dead," I told him, though I hadn't meant to be so blunt. "She died in childbirth." I set my fork on my plate. "She didn't teach me anything."

Coltar squeezed his eyes closed and it looked like he was in pain. He hadn't known. This wasn't something I thought a person could fake. "I'm really sorry to hear that, Elizabeth. Your mother was... She was special."

Orin's eyes narrowed on Coltar. "Wouldn't you know that? If Audrey was in contact with you—"

"I'm not in contact with Audrey. I haven't even spoken to her in..." He looked at me. "In at least twenty-one years. She let me know you were coming by calling someone else, who told another person... It was a long chain between her and me. They told me that you were coming to look for me and that it was for your protection. When I heard that, I knew I couldn't ignore or hide from you. Now." He folded his hands in front of himself. "What do you need me to protect you from when you have him?" He nodded toward Orin.

"She doesn't *need* you," Orin snapped. "I've kept her safe this long and I'll continue to keep her safe."

Coltar picked up his fork and took a bite of the chicken, something I'd yet to do. "I wasn't questioning that. I'm sure you're more than capable. Most werewolves are." So he knew what Orin was, yet we hadn't told him. "But there has to be more, right? If, after all of these years, you've come looking for me." He was talking to me, not to Orin.

"I—"

"Before we get to that." Orin gave me a pointed

look that I knew meant I should just go with what he's saying. "Why don't we focus on the other things? Elizabeth didn't know that her father—Henry Davis—wasn't her father until very recently. As in days ago. I'm sure she has questions."

Coltar nodded and sat back in his chair. His plate was almost emptied, though I'd barely noticed him eating, while I'd taken only a few bites, but that was all I was going to be able to. My stomach was in too much turmoil to eat any more.

"Are we all finished?" Coltar asked.

I nodded and Orin's plate was almost empty as well. The men ate quickly, I guess.

"Leave these here," Coltar said. "I'll clean up after we're done talking."

He led us to the main room and started a fire in the fireplace. The later in the day it got, the cooler the air became. The heat coming from the fire as it built felt good and made the room more homey.

"Your mother and I came here," he told me, sitting on the chair nearest the sofa where Orin and I sat. "We were just kids ourselves." His eyes had a far-off look to them.

"How did you two meet?" I asked.

"By chance," he said. "Simply by chance. We were both in town. I wasn't supposed to be and she came hurrying around the corner of a store and slammed into me so hard, she knocked me off my feet."

I couldn't help but smile. "She knocked you off your feet? Are you speaking metaphorically?"

He chuckled. "No. Werewolves are strong." He glanced at Orin. "I don't think I have to tell you that." He swallowed hard. "But her smile was infectious and I knew she was a shifter. That alone meant I was supposed to stay away from her. But I couldn't." Sadness tugged at the corners of his gray eyes. "I should've."

"Why?" Orin asked. "Why would you have to stay away from her? Isn't the whole point of your being to impregnate women?"

Coltar scowled and I wanted to dig my fingernails into my husband's arm. He didn't have to be so blunt about it.

"No," Coltar answered. "It's not the whole point. But yes, that's something an incubus does. It was different with Thora because I was in love with her. She was the only woman I've ever fallen in love with and letting her go was the hardest thing I've ever done. But it was the best thing for Elizabeth."

"I have so many questions," I told him. "What do you mean, the only woman you've fallen in love with? Don't you have a wife? You don't love her? Why was it best for me? Did you know I was a girl? Did you know she was going to name me Elizabeth?"

"I do love my wife. But I've never been in love with her. It's all right." He held a hand up to stop the other questions that I had. "She's not in love with me, either. We were friends and both were expected to marry, so we decided to marry each other. The love of her life was killed in a fight with another demon." He moved to the edge of his seat and folded his hands before him. "And yes, I knew you were going to be a girl. Your mother told me. I don't know how she knew, but I believed her. And yes, she told me she was going to name you Elizabeth, after her mother."

So their relationship had been a real one. They had actually been in love, which meant my mother had known true love, even though she'd died so young.

"She's also the one who saw my death," he confessed. "She touched me and saw that I was going to die."

I furrowed my brows. "How? I see death sometimes, but it's right before it happens."

"She had practice, Elizabeth. That means she could see it a little further out. But she saw that my people would kill me for keeping a part incubus, wolf shifter banshee. We knew what would happen even if it wasn't going to happen until after you were born. So we decided she should run."

"Orin's mother didn't seem to think I'm a succubus. They said that's a female..." I waved my hands at him. "You."

"It is a female me, but no. You wouldn't be." He watched me out of the corner of his eye with one eyebrow slightly raised. "You couldn't be mixed with anything else. A succubus is the result of an incubus and succubus pairing, or replacing one with a full human. You have no human blood at all. It wouldn't work. But he would know that, wouldn't he?"

The *he* in question was Orin and yes, he did know that.

"How did this happen?" Coltar waved a finger between the two of us.

Orin and I told him together. Of him following his mate's call and it turning out to be me. We didn't leave any details out, either. Even if Orin wanted to, I didn't. So unless Orin specifically told me not to share something, I was going to share. This was the only chance I'd had with a blood relative other than Audrey and she couldn't tell me everything. She hadn't known everything.

"Why did you think she was human?" Coltar asked Orin. "Could you not sense more?"

"I sensed some of it," he told him after a moment of contemplation. "There was something different, but I had no reason to believe it."

"Right." Coltar moved over to the fire and stoked it with the fire poker. "Well, a succubus is meant to lure men to sex for procreation. But you're married, right?"

I nodded. "Yes. But I do seem to be able to... lure him into things." My cheeks heated. I couldn't believe I'd just said that in front of a basic stranger. He might've been my father, but if my father's people were so open, then I was going to be.

Coltar laughed loudly. "Oh, sweetheart. I don't think that has anything to do with being a succubus. Like I said, it wouldn't work that way."

Orin ran his hand up and then down my back. "I told you that had nothing to do with it."

On to the next subject before I burned from embarrassment.

"What am I protecting you from?" Coltar asked. "Outside of my family?"

Now it was Orin's turn to explain that my mother's pack was out to claim me and mate me as their own in the hope that I'd be able to produce babies for the pack. He didn't spare a detail. When he mentioned Phillip, the guilt hit me like running into a wall. Pushing that aside, I continued to listen.

"They aren't even being picky about who mates with her, are they?" he asked.

"No." It was one word, but that single answer conveyed how murderous it made Orin. "On top of that, my pack has their own enemies to fight and one tried to get to Elizabeth. I have no doubt he would've killed her slowly to get back at us."

"What happened to him?"

"I ripped his throat out."

"Why do you have enemies?"

"Power. My family is the head of the packs in our area. Not everyone loves that."

Coltar snorted. "Yeah. My family has that problem, too."

The sun had begun to set, so Coltar turned on lights as we continued to talk. He told me a little about his family, though not too much. It was as if he didn't want to share all of their secrets. Then he asked me a thousand questions about growing up. At first, I was going to keep back details of Henry Davis ruling with a heavy hand, but then I didn't. I told Coltar everything, including what Audrey had told me about Henry wanting someone beautiful on his arm.

The muscle in Coltar's jaw hardened. "I'd like to be angry with him," he said. "And I am for the way he treated you, but he did take you on when I couldn't." His gray eyes met mine. "For that, I have to be thankful. He got you here, which means he protected you."

"He did." That much was true. Henry Davis hadn't let anything bad happen to me, but he would have. He would've left me to be Noah Underwood's plaything if Orin hadn't stepped in.

"Do you have a telephone here?" Orin asked suddenly.

"Not at the house. There's one down at the corner." He tossed Orin the keys to his car. "You can use that."

It made sense for him not to have a phone here at the house. Then people would know someone was here. Others could find out. If this was supposed to be safe, then it was best to be cut off from the world.

Coltar told me more about my mother from when he'd known her. He hadn't known exactly when I'd been born, and he'd had no idea she had died until I'd told him. That was something he'd regret forever, he said. Not seeing Thora one more time before she died.

It was easy to talk to him and if Orin had left me alone with the man, Coltar must've earned his trust.

Twenty minutes later, Orin was back with a severe, hard look on his face.

Something was wrong. Something was very wrong.

I hurried over to him. "What is it? What's happened?"

"I called my parents." Something he must've sensed needed to be done. "I'm sorry, Elizabeth. Henry Davis is dead."

Chapter Fifteen

STARING at the ceiling as I lay in bed with my husband in a house that my biological father had brought me to while thinking about the man who'd raised me being dead, I tried to come up with one good memory of Henry Davis. There wasn't a single one.

If you counted the fact that he'd kept me fed and clothed out of obligation and how it would look if he'd let his own supposed daughter starve, then sure. Great memories.

I didn't count those.

"You need to get some sleep," Orin murmured from next to me, sounding as tired as I felt, but my brain wouldn't shut off.

"I know, but I can't. I can't stop thinking about

him." Though I didn't want to confess the worst part, I would because this was Orin next to me. "I feel bad."

"What?"

"I feel bad that I don't feel worse." I turned on the bed so that I could face him. Orin was next to me without a shirt on, on his back, but his head was turned to look at me. "He did raise me. He was awful to me, but he could've tossed me aside after my mother died. Yet he didn't and I don't know why if he knew I wasn't his."

Orin reached a hand out to cup my cheek. His hands were strong, but when he touched me, they were so gentle. "He doesn't deserve your tears, Elizabeth."

"I know. But I feel bad that I'm not shedding them." I paused. "We need to know who killed him."

It could've been morbid curiosity, but with everything going on, we had to know.

"My brothers are on it. They'll find out." He tucked me under his arm so my body could melt into his warmth. "Now, are you going to get some sleep or do I need to help you with that?"

I let my hand roam his bare chest, the hard muscles comforting me. "We just met Coltar. I can't do that here right now."

He snorted. "But a crowded train is fine."

My skin lit on fire. He was right. That had been so out of character for me, but it was what had been needed at the time. Tonight, just being beside him was going to have to be enough.

After all, I'd gotten these heightened senses from somewhere. The last thing I wanted to think about was my real father hearing me with Orin. That wasn't the solution tonight.

Having Orin beside me made it easier to drift off to sleep.

In the morning, the smell of breakfast filled the air before I ever got out of bed.

Orin threw the covers off himself and swung his legs over the side of the bed. "I thought he said he doesn't cook much."

"I don't know." Then the sound of a second voice brought the both of us to a stop. "Who could that be?" I whispered.

Orin shrugged then went back to getting himself dressed. I did the same.

We went down the stairs to the kitchen together. My stomach made a loud sound the closer we got. I hadn't eaten properly in so long that I couldn't remember my last meal. Picking at what I'd taken last night didn't count.

"Did we wake you?" Coltar asked when he saw us.

"The bacon did," I told him because that was what was most fragrant.

He came to a stop in front of me. "I thought you'd be hungry," he said, watching me carefully. "You barely ate last night."

It was odd having someone other than Orin, or maybe my best friend Olivia, care at all about my needs and I wasn't sure I totally trusted it. The woman behind him cleared her throat, making him step aside.

This woman was young, probably five years younger than I was, which would've made her around sixteen. She was taller than me with the most beautiful brown hair and the same gray eyes Coltar had.

"Dad," she whisper-yelled.

"Oh, right. Sorry. Elizabeth, this is my daughter Meredith."

Which made her my sister. Half-sister, anyway.

"It's nice to meet you," I told her, but I questioned Coltar with my eyes. Before I could put words to that question, I was hit with a stronger force than Meredith should've been able to provide. She was solid and with her arms wrapped around my shoulders, holding me so tightly, I could barely breathe.

Orin's growl erupted, causing Coltar to reach out and pull Meredith gently away from me.

"Let her breathe," he told her.

"I'm sorry," she said to me. "I've always wanted a sister."

Coltar motioned to the table, so Orin and I sat down, breakfast already laid out.

"You don't have any sisters?" I asked as Orin held a bowl of scrambled eggs for me to serve myself from because Coltar hadn't told us much about his family.

"I have you," she said excitedly. Clearly, she knew more than I did because I hadn't even known he had another daughter, yet she knew about me. "Otherwise... Ugh." She groaned. "Three older brothers."

"I asked Meredith to come here today to help me with breakfast. I hope you don't mind."

When I sunk my teeth into the first piece of bacon and the flavor exploded in my mouth, I said, "I don't mind." Once I'd chewed that down, I asked what I'd wanted to ask since I'd gotten here and since she was now with us, that meant he'd decided to trust us with more, I thought. "So you have four kids?"

"Five," he corrected me. "I've never kept the

knowledge of you from them. They all know. My larger family also knows. It wasn't something I could keep quiet long, but it was fine because I knew they wouldn't find you."

Suddenly, I had four siblings after a lifetime of having none.

"How did you know?"

Coltar's eyes met mine. "I knew." Which meant I wasn't going to get more of an explanation right now.

"I'm so excited," Meredith squealed.

"She's very excited," Coltar said with a dead-panned tone and the corners of his mouth fighting to turn up.

"I see that."

"You married a shifter?" she asked, coming toward me so close that it was as if she didn't under-stand personal boundaries.

"Yes."

"What's that like? I've heard about shifters, but I don't think I've met any." She turned to our father. "Dad?"

"No." But his eyes stayed on me the entire time. That was something I'd noticed last night. He watched me like a hawk watched a mouse it was preparing to grab. It took me a while to figure out that it was just how a father would watch a daughter, especially one he'd just met.

"I've never met one," Meredith said.

"You can't say that now," Orin told her. The fact that he'd grown up with a literal pack of siblings meant he was far better able to handle this right now.

"So if they know about me," I said, "does that mean I get to know about them?"

Coltar nodded. "My wife, Caroline, and I have Theo, Mason, and Arlo in that order and then Meredith is the youngest."

"Theo's the oldest?" I asked. He nodded. "How old is he?"

Realization set in. He knew exactly what I was asking.

"He'll be twenty-one in a few months."

Which meant he'd gone right from my mother to his wife. How much could he have loved my mother if he could do that? Could Orin do that? Go from me directly to another woman's bed?

The mere thought of it made my stomach hurt and breakfast was done for me. I pushed the plate away from me and Orin set his hand on mine, probably to calm me.

"How could you say that you loved my mother if you went from her to your wife so quickly?"

"I explained that," Coltar said, glancing at Meredith and then back at me. "I loved Thora. She's the only woman I've ever loved." Meredith sat roughly back against the chair and pushed the food around her plate. "The kids know everything. I loved her and you. But Caroline was my best friend, so when we knew we were both expected to marry to produce more of us, we decided to do that. There are worse marriages to be had than that with your best friend."

He wasn't wrong there. I'd seen so many loveless marriages in my father's society that at least if you were with your best friend, you'd love them. Even if it wasn't in a romantic way.

"I'm sorry," I told him. "I shouldn't have said that. I just... I didn't get to know her and I always hoped that she was loved."

"She was," Coltar told me and the conviction behind his words made me believe him.

I was on the verge of asking more questions about his family when he suddenly stood, as did Meredith.

Orin furrowed his brows then jumped up. "Wait." But I still had no idea what was happening. Orin's chair hit the ground as he tried to get to the door before the rush of Coltar and his daughter.

That was when I heard something. Or rather someone.

"Who are you?" Coltar yelled from outside. Then something hit the dirt.

A growl erupted before I could make it out the door. With all of them yelling, I couldn't make out the words.

Finally, I was able to see clearly.

Coltar had Ivan on the ground by his neck with Meredith looking over, a light glow coming from both of their eyes. Orin was an arm's length away, being held there by Coltar.

"Wait!" I called out then ran toward them. "Wait!"

That was what got Coltar's attention.

"That's Ivan," I said, slightly out of breath. "Orin's brother."

"As I've told you twice now," Orin said menacingly, "let go of my brother before I have to end you."

Coltar snorted but lowered his arm from Orin and removed his hand from Ivan's neck as the glow in his eyes slowly faded away. That glow had to be the demon inside of him. There was no other explanation that would've made sense.

"How did you find us?" he asked once Ivan was back on his feet.

"It's a wolf thing." And that was all the explanation that anyone would be getting. The Vilkatas pack wasn't about to share any of their secrets with anyone outside of the pack. I only knew because Orin had explained it to me once. That didn't mean I understood it.

"Why are you here?" Coltar demanded.

"I came for them." Ivan sounded much calmer than he had before. "With Henry Davis dead, we have some theories. Trust me. I don't want to be here any more than you want me to be."

Coltar raised an eyebrow but stood there, watching Ivan with narrow eyes, as if he were trying to figure out the man's intentions.

Maybe he was. After all, that was a thing for an incubus, right? They could basically smell whether or not someone meant harm.

"You don't intend to try to kill me," Coltar said, as if this were a foregone conclusion. "However, I can sense that I shouldn't trust you around Elizabeth." He moved closer, his jaw set. "That means you have to leave. Now."

It was a showdown between werewolf and incubus. I wasn't sure who would win, but I also didn't want to find out.

Once I was close enough, I said, "Ivan hates me, but he won't hurt me."

"How can you be so sure?"

I swallowed hard. "Because he's already had the chance to and he didn't take it. It would hurt his brother."

Coltar stood there another couple of seconds, then gave a slight nod and stepped away. "Then let's get into the house before someone sees us."

Once we were inside and introductions were made, Ivan stayed on his feet, as if he were worried he'd have to run or respond at any moment.

"What're you doing here?" Coltar asked him.

"I told you." Ivan folded his arms over his chest, looking incredibly intimidating. "I came for them."

"You went to Davis's house?" Orin asked, putting an end to Coltar's questioning.

"Yes." His eyes momentarily flitted to me. "It was the Balodis. Of that, we have no doubt."

"How do you know?" I asked, but I was unlikely to get an answer.

As if I weren't there at all, Ivan continued. "There was a message. *Bring us Elizabeth.*"

Everything about Orin tightened in alert. He was taller, his muscles like brick. "What?"

Ivan loosened his arms. "We tracked one down.

Got him to talk." But the way he scanned over to Coltar and Meredith told me he wasn't sure if he should say anything else in front of them.

"Go ahead," Orin urged.

"They're not going to stop. Not until they get her. The sniveling fool we grabbed said that Davis won't be the last."

I furrowed my brows. What did that mean? They wouldn't stop? Stop what? Trying to get me? We'd already known that.

"Elizabeth." Coltar gently grabbed my arms, snapping me out of my own thoughts. "Is there anyone else that you care about? I'm sure Audrey is covered."

"No." Orin was the only person in my life. "I didn't love my father. Why would they think this would do anything?"

"Likely, it's just a message. Them showing that they aren't afraid to kill to get to you."

Well, I didn't want innocent people to die, of course, but my father had been far from innocent. "Wait," I said too loudly, then I hurried to Orin. "Olivia. She's the only other person. She doesn't know about any of this. If they know about her..." Tears welled up in my eyes. "I can't let anything happen to her. She doesn't deserve that."

"I can have the pack protect her."

"We're spread pretty thin, brother," Ivan countered.

"We have to go," I told him more seriously. Just the fact that Olivia had been my friend since we'd been kids was putting her in danger. She'd been the only one who'd been there for me most of my life. I couldn't let this happen.

"I don't want you anywhere near there," Orin insisted.

"We don't have a choice."

In my mind, we didn't. I'd have to hope that I had better control of my own powers than I thought I did. It was the only way to manage all of this.

"She's right," Ivan said, agreeing with me for the first time since I'd met him. "We can't do it all and will need the entire pack as it is. You two can't hide out here and leave us to fight your battle."

"It's *our* battle. All of ours," Orin countered. He sighed. "But you're right. We have to go back. You don't, Elizabeth. We can leave you here." Though his skin looked suddenly gray at the idea.

Leaving me behind had never been an option before and yet... now he was suggesting it.

"She can't stay here," Coltar told them. I had

been on the verge of arguing the point myself, but him rejecting me was somewhat of a surprise.

When we'd come here, I hadn't imagined I'd be welcomed with open arms, given what I'd learned about his family. Yet I also didn't think he'd push me back out into the world without consideration for my safety.

"Elizabeth," Coltar said, taking command of the room. Something in the way his voice reverberated off the walls. "I'd love to keep you here, but my family wouldn't take this well. Your brothers and my wife would, but the rest of the nest... no. There's only one thing I can do to keep you safe."

Each of his hands clasped the sides of my head roughly, sending shots of electricity through me and making me fall to my knees. I yelled at the pain and could hear both Orin and Ivan but couldn't understand what they were saying. The pulses kept coming. Tears streamed down my face as I tried to catch my breath.

Then he broke the connection. I was on my hands and knees with Orin wrapping a strong arm around me.

"You just made a fatal mistake," Orin told him once he'd lifted me to my feet.

Coltar's eyes stayed focused on me and it was

like I could hear what he was thinking. This wasn't the case with everyone. Only him. "No. I gave her something that might help her survive."

And then I understood.

I'd sucked the energy from the man in the hotel without having any clue as to how I'd done it. Now, I understood what I needed to do.

This would let me protect myself.

"We should go," I whispered.

"Elizabeth?" Orin searched my face for signs that I was all right, so I gave him a small, reassuring smile.

"The brothers will meet us there," Ivan said.

Now we were going home. It just wasn't how I'd expected we'd be doing it.

Chapter Sixteen

WE'D BARELY DROPPED our bags at our house before we were headed to find Olivia. Of course, Orin wasn't going to let me go alone. Before we turned down her street, I had a change of plans.

"Can we go to my father's house first?" I asked.

It was weird calling him that now, knowing that he wasn't my father, but I wasn't sure what else to call him. That was how I'd thought of him my entire life. Was I now going to call Coltar "Father"? "Dad," as Meredith did? It was all too confusing.

"I don't think that's a good idea," Orin said, but he turned the car away from Olivia's house and toward my father's.

"I need to go there," I told him. "I don't know

why." And he accepted that answer. After Coltar had given me the energy boost, Orin wanted to know exactly what happened, but I couldn't explain it to him. I assured him I was fine and that was the best I could do. I tried my best.

He took the long driveway slowly, as if doing so would change my mind. I couldn't explain why I needed to see the place, but I did.

When we got to the front door, I lifted my hand to knock, as I would have any other time I'd been here since I'd left with Orin. Granted, it'd been very few times, but after that point, I couldn't see it as my home. Hell, before that, I'd only seen it as my home because I'd had to live there. But then I dropped my hand and stepped inside.

"Elizabeth." Mrs. Atherton, my father's housekeeper and my former nanny, came hurrying toward me with open arms. She wrapped them around me and squeezed. "I'm sorry you're back under these circumstances. It's a lot for you to deal with."

That was right. She wouldn't have been comforting me about my father's death because as the housekeeper who'd been here all the time, she knew how my father had been. She knew that there hadn't been any love lost between the two of us.

"What do you mean?" I asked.

"Well, as his only living relative..." She let those words trail off and honestly, that wasn't something I'd thought about. "His lawyer has already called asking for updated information for you. I'm sure you'll hear from him soon." Mrs. Atherton turned toward Orin, giving him a nod as she said, "Mr. Vilkatas."

Did... Did she think I was going to manage my father's affairs? No way. His lawyer could do that, given that he'd probably known my father better than I had.

"It happened here," she whispered. "In the back garden. Mr. Pepper found him." That was my father's groundkeeper and had been for years. "He's taken care of everything back here." A pregnant pause pushed out for too long. Was she waiting for a response from me?

"What can I do for you?" she finally asked.

"Nothing, Mrs. Atherton. I had to come... I don't know why."

She nodded, as if that explanation made perfect sense, but I didn't see how it could. It didn't to me. Orin had my fingers threaded through his while he held my hand and it was all the support I could've stood right then.

I wasn't sad about my father's death, exactly. Did

I feel bad that he'd been murdered because of me? Yes. I wouldn't want that for anyone, but I didn't feel the sense of loss that others would have felt when losing their fathers.

"Elizabeth," Orin urged.

"Right." Then I turned back to Mrs. Atherton. "Is the household managed?"

"Yes. I have access to the household funds and was assured that wouldn't change in the short term. Decisions would have to be made, of course, but not today. You have plenty of time."

I raised an eyebrow. "Decisions?"

"Well, yes. For example, will you be keeping the house? Moving here? Again, this isn't something you have to deal with today." I had to deal with? It still didn't make sense. She stepped closer. "As his only heir."

Well... damn.

She was right. My father didn't have any family still living and to everyone else, it would look like I was his heir. Though none of us knew exactly how he'd set up his will.

"I... We have to go, Mrs. Atherton, but I'll check back with you soon."

"Of course, dear. Of course."

Orin let me go out in front of him then closed the door behind him.

We were out in the sunlight and the weather was mild, so I soaked up the rays and took in a deep breath of fresh air. Inside that house, I'd felt like I'd been suffocating.

"Are they going to expect me to make decisions?" I spun around to face him. "I can't make decisions for that man, Orin. Even if he was killed because of me. He hated me. I had no warm feelings for him. I'm not the best person to decide how he's sent off from this world."

"Hey, hey, hey," he said quickly, running his hands down and then up my arms. "You don't have to do anything you don't want to. A man like your father I'm sure already had his plans laid out. I don't think you'll have to do anything."

"What if I do?" My eyes burned with the threat of tears. Not for my father, but because of the panic rising in my chest.

"Then I'll do it for you. Isn't that the thing? The husband takes over?"

At least that made me laugh and I dropped my forehead against his chest briefly before standing up straight. "All right. Now to go talk to Olivia. I don't know what we're going to say."

"Whatever we have to, right?"

Right. I wanted Olivia to get her family out of town for a while. At least until the threat passed. Or at the very least, we were going to have to do something to convince people she meant nothing to me. It was possible that they didn't even know about her, given I'd barely seen her since Orin had come to town. She'd been busy with her engagement and wedding at that time. After that, she'd wanted kids right away and I had heard she was pregnant now, but I hadn't seen her.

"We can't go to her house," I said. "What if it's being watched? Is that something they'd do?"

"Possibly. We'll call her and have her meet us. You'll have to convince her."

So I did.

Orin stopped on Main Street, leaving me to hurry to the phone to call her house. After too long, her housekeeper answered and after a while, Olivia came on the line.

"Elizabeth?" she asked in surprise.

"Hello, Olivia."

"I haven't heard from you in forever."

"I know. It's been too long and I'm sorry for that." I swallowed hard. "I've been very busy. Listen, could you meet me for a few minutes?"

"Today's not the best day," she told me, but that wasn't going to work.

"It's very important," I told her. "I... I just got back to town today because my father..."

"Oh, yes, Elizabeth. I'm so sorry. I did hear about that this morning. Awful business. Where should I meet you?"

I told her to meet me at the corner near the pharmacy. It was close enough that we could go into the nearby woods if we needed to prove anything to her.

That sounded so weird to my ears.

"Elizabeth!" she called out a short while later, causing me to spin around and rush into her arms. "I'm so sorry about your father. I know you didn't have the best relationship. He could be a difficult man, but I'm sorry."

"Thank you." I gave her one last squeeze before pulling back and setting my hands on her belly, thankful that I didn't see her death. If anything, it wasn't imminent. "And congratulations."

"It's still early," she whispered. She was right. It was early. If I didn't know her so well, I might not have noticed. "Now, what did you need me for so urgently?" She looped her arm through mine and started walking. "I see your husband right there."

Orin had stayed back slightly to not scare her off

and to allow me this small moment of friend time, given that it was going to be my last for who-knew-how-long.

"Actually, we both needed to talk to you." I stopped so Orin could join us. "You know what happened to my father, right?"

"Yes. He died." Her hazel eyes were round and as large as they could possibly be. This was her scared.

"You don't have to be afraid," I told her. "Not of us. But my father was… murdered, Olivia."

Her hand flew to her chest in surprise. "What? That doesn't happen here. This is a safe city."

"I know. Normally, it doesn't, but he was killed…" I took a deep breath and blew it out slowly. "He was killed because someone was looking for me."

"What?" She grabbed my arms tightly. "Are you all right?"

"Yes. It's a long story and will sound unbelievable."

"I'll believe you, Lizzie. You wouldn't lie to me. We've known each other too long."

Good. That at least made me feel somewhat better. This might be easier than I'd been thinking.

"My mother's family has been looking for me. They want me to join them."

She furrowed her brows. "Join them for what?"

"That's not important." And there was enough that I was going to tell her that would shock her. I didn't want to include that. "But they'll stop at nothing to get to me. That's why they killed him. They thought hurting someone I loved would bring me out of the woodwork."

"Which it did," Orin said under his breath, to which I scowled.

"You didn't love him, though."

"Exactly." Then I waited, hoping that she'd put the pieces together and I saw the moment it happened on her face. Those hazel eyes grew again and her lips parted.

"Are you saying that I'm in danger?" Her voice was too high to be considered normal.

"I don't know. But that's our fear."

"Is there somewhere you could go?" Orin asked her. "Out of town for a while?"

"I don't know. I'd have to ask my husband."

"It's really important," I told her. "If you could go away for a little while, then I'd know you're safe."

"What's going on?" she demanded. "There's something you're not telling me."

I took a breath again. "I don't think you'll believe me."

"Lizzie," she snapped. "Stop saying that. You're my best friend. It doesn't matter if we haven't talked in a while. It's always been you. If you tell me, I'll believe you."

Well, there was nothing else to do but try. "My mother wasn't human. She was part werewolf shifter and part banshee."

"You're joking, right? I don't believe that..." Then she snapped her lips closed when she realized what she'd said. "I believe you. But... what does that mean?"

"I can't explain it all to you, but Henry Davis wasn't my father. Not my real father. My mother was already pregnant when they met. My real father is an incubus. These are things you've probably never heard of, but it's true."

"That makes you..."

"A wolf, banshee, incubus combination. I don't understand it all yet, either, Olivia. But Orin is a werewolf shifter and that's why he showed up at that ball. He was searching for his mate and it turned out to be me."

She shook her head slowly. "I feel like I should sit down. I can't believe this is happening."

"I couldn't believe it, either, but this is where we're at."

She eyed Orin suspiciously. "This isn't all a sick joke, is it?" I shook my head. "If you're a... wolf shifter, banshee, incubus, does that mean you have supernatural powers?"

"Yes."

"Can you show me?"

I snickered. This was my best friend talking. "None of mine are impressive or something I can show you."

"They're very impressive," Orin countered, which reminded me that he could show her.

"He can show you," I offered. "It's... startling at first, but he can show you. We'd have to go over to the trees, though. No one else can see him."

She nodded like an excited kid on Christmas morning. At the very least, I knew she trusted me. Right now, she was trusting me that I wasn't crazy talking about all of these supernatural creatures and maybe she was humoring me. Maybe deep down, she didn't believe me but wouldn't say it.

In a moment, she wouldn't be able to deny it.

"He has to... undress," I said. Her eyes bulged and she turned away. "I'll let you know when he's done."

He could've shifted in his clothes, but then he'd be left with nothing to wear home. This was better.

"All right. You can turn around."

"Lizzie." She gasped.

Orin was standing a little away from us without any clothes on, but he was holding his pants in front of his... manly parts so Olivia couldn't see anything inappropriate. But then again, in society, seeing him without the shirt right now was inappropriate.

"I want you to see it so you don't think we've pulled a prank on you."

She sighed and then Orin did his thing.

With each part of the transformation, Olivia's fingers dug harder into my arm. Orin did it slowly so she wouldn't miss a thing. His pants floated to the ground as the beast I knew as my husband was before us.

And the circulation in my arm was cut off by Olivia's hands.

"Lizzie, what is that?" She squealed.

"I told you." I wiggled my arm out of her grasp. "He's a wolf shifter. He's not going to hurt us."

She cocked her head to the side. "Is that... fur? It looks soft. Can I touch it?"

Orin growled as I said, "You definitely can't touch it." Given his reaction when I touched him, I wasn't willing for anyone else to make him feel that. Whether he was all right with it or not. "Now let's turn around so he can get dressed."

Once our backs were to him, Orin began to change back, a stick snapping under his weight. Olivia and I began to slowly walk in the opposite direction.

"And you think I could be in danger?" she asked.

"I worry that you are. Just by knowing me. If anyone asks, Olivia, I need you to say you don't know me."

"But people know we're friends."

"I know. I just don't think that my mother's family will ask around. Or I hope they won't." We were back out in the sunlight when we stopped. "So, can you leave town for a while?"

She sighed. "Charles's father just bought a hotel in New York City. Charles is going there to get things settled. I could go with him and extend the stay. Tell him it's a getaway before the baby comes."

"How long do you think you can get him to stay?"

"I don't know, but as long as I can," she said. Orin joined us right then. "I'll call you in a few weeks to see if it's safe to come back."

That was the best I could hope for.

If nothing else happened, I could at least say I'd done everything I could to keep my best friend safe.

Chapter Seventeen

With Olivia heading off to New York, there wasn't much we could do right now. Orin and his brothers wanted to form a plan and see whom they could draw out. But for tonight, Orin and I were going to sleep in our own bed and I was looking forward to it.

With everything I'd done today, dinner time arrived and I hadn't even thought about what I was going to make. Orin and his brothers were going to be hungry. The kitchen was mostly empty because of the fact that we'd been gone for a while. I couldn't exactly run to the market to buy supplies. Daniel had already gotten us a few necessities since they'd been back here longer than we had.

I'd eaten so poorly these last days that it was

catching up to me. Right as I was about to ask Roman what we should do—he was the one tasked with watching me right now since I was not to be left alone—the front door opened. The fact that Roman didn't react was how I knew this wasn't an attack. The sound of many excited voices filled my house. I hurried out of the kitchen to find Anton, Emmi, and Karina coming through with bags in their hands.

Karina rushed over to me. "I'm so happy to see you. Are you all right?" She pulled back and looked me over. "You seem all right."

"I'm fine. What are you doing here?"

"It was always the plan for us to come. Diana and Aras stayed back. As you know, Aras can't fight and we're keeping Diana as safe as we can, at least for now."

"They're taking care of things back home," Emmi added. "Now, we need to start dinner."

At least they'd come prepared. Karina and Emmi began unpacking the sacks while Anton went over to Roman, I guessed for an update, so I went to the kitchen, wanting to help where I could.

"I hope you don't find this too odd," Emmi started. "But we decided to have steak and eggs for dinner."

"With potatoes," Karina added.

Steak and eggs were normally a breakfast meal, but right now, I would've eaten anything.

While they worked—after shooing me away—I filled them in on meeting Coltar and going to my father's house. Then about getting Olivia to leave. Hopefully, they'd leave tonight or in the morning. In society, trips were typically planned out in advance. You wouldn't catch a society wife packing up and leaving on a whim.

"The rest of the pack is coming," Karina told me. "They've staggered leaving the packhouse so that hopefully no one will be attacked on the way. We weren't."

"The entire pack?" I wasn't sure what that meant. To me, the entire pack was the parents, the sons, and their wives—not to mention poor little Ruby and baby Daniel. The only childred in the middle of all of this.

"Yeah. Don't worry. You're not going to meet any of them, probably. They're going to lurk since that's what we do best, but Anton wants to put an end to this once and for all."

"The Balodis's power has grown recently," Emmi explained. "As has their pack, and no one's sure why. They're still having breeding problems, which we now know they blame on your grandmother."

"For bringing banshee blood into the line," Karina clarified.

"But they were having problems before that." Emmi dropped a few steaks into some pans. I hadn't been paying close enough attention to figure out what they'd gotten done. "Don't worry, dear. We're going to end this. Then you and my son can get on with your lives."

"And give her some more grandbabies." Karina did her best to mimic Emmi's voice, which got her swatted with a spoon. "Ouch." She giggled.

"Wait." I held up one finger. "Why do I have to get busy giving her grandbabies? You've been married longer."

"Barely." It was then I realized that I didn't know how long any of them had been married or together, or anything about them. "We haven't been married a year yet."

So Karina had been newly wed when I'd met her. She and Roman had acted like they'd been together for a long time.

"I knew Roman since we were kids. He was annoying..." She shrugged. "Until he wasn't."

"So you grew up together?"

She nodded. "My family is part of the Vilkatas pack. Not related by blood, but pack mates by oath.

My grandfather promised fealty to Roman's grandfather a long time ago. See..." She continued to work as she spoke. "My blood pack had gotten too small, which left us open to attack. When a pack gets too small, it's going to be absorbed into another, larger pack. My grandfather being our alpha would be the one to make the choice, but we could either be conquered or make an alliance. And until now, no one would threaten the Vilkatas pack. It wasn't really a decision he wrestled with."

"Why until now?"

"Because of you," Emmi said, but there was no harshness in her words. "It wouldn't be hard to figure out that our focus has been elsewhere because of you. If they now know you are one of a kind... it'll be surprising if more packs don't make a move for you in the hopes that you being of wolf blood, along with the other supernatural blood, would make you resistant to whatever has been killing their women."

I swallowed hard and my stomach turned. "Is that... happening in your pack?"

"Hell no." Emmi laughed loudly. "We're all as healthy as horses. Breeding has never been an issue. You'll see eventually. Anton's mother had twelve kids. There are eleven of his brothers and sisters in the pack. They each had at least four kids. So far, in their generation, all the babies and mothers are healthy, like Ruby and Diana." She turned to me with a more serious look on her face. "I know Diana has been a bit of a pill since you met her and I don't think that's likely to change anytime soon. But I promise you, she's a good person deep down. She just has experiences none of us can understand that made her hate humans."

Karina nodded, then mouthed, *I'll tell you later.* Having at least one friend in this family made being here so much easier.

"And Aras is just a bitch," Karina said. I slapped a hand over my mouth to keep from laughing, both because she'd said that in front of her mother-in-law and because she'd said it at all.

"I'd appreciate you not speaking about my wife that way," Daniel said, making me jump. With all of them around, I found that I lowered my guard and didn't listen as hard, so he'd been able to sneak up on me.

"But we all know it's true," Karina replied.

"Roman," he barked out. "Come handle your woman."

Heavy thuds allowed me to track Roman and Anton until they came into the kitchen.

"Why?" Roman asked. "What'd she do?"

"She said my wife is a bitch."

Roman furrowed my brows. "But she is."

Now I had to bite my lips together. This was the most relaxed and playful I'd ever seen this family. It was like they'd decided to let their collective guard down around me, as if they'd finally accepted that I was part of the family, even if certain members didn't necessarily like that fact. Orin wasn't giving me up any more than they'd give up their wives. They had to accept it and I hoped this was the first step in doing that.

"Aras and Diana aren't coming at all?" I asked to clarify. It would have been fine if they were, but I wanted to be really clear about this.

"No," Emmi answered as the rest of them fell silent. "When one of us is pregnant, we don't fight. Continuing the line is the most important thing for that woman at that time. We can't risk Aras being hurt in any way."

"I'm glad," I told her. "I don't want anyone hurt at all."

Daniel snorted but didn't say anything.

"And for now," Emmi continued while narrowing her eyes on Daniel in a pointed look, "we're going to let Diana work through her grief. If necessary, she would come and leave Ruby and

Daniel Jr. with Aras, but we will be just fine without her."

Diana might've hated me even before her husband had died to protect me, but in no world did I want her to be hurt or for Ruby to be an orphan. No matter how much loving family she had around her.

"What's going on in here?" Orin came through the door, his clothes disheveled the way they often were after he'd been out on a run. Suddenly, I wanted to know why his brothers had come back before him.

"Emmi was just explaining why Diana and Aras aren't here," Karina told him. "And why we're going to end this so that Elizabeth can get busy giving Emmi some grandbabies."

Orin's gaze found mine quickly. That was something we'd only really talked about once. He hadn't known then how my mother's bloodline would affect the whole childbirth thing. For her, it had killed her. For me... who knew? I was part incubus, after all, and apparently, one of their purposes was to procreate. Maybe that meant babies with that blood were protected?

It was all too much to think about.

There was one thing I did know, though. There

was no scenario in which Orin would let me put myself at risk for a baby the way my mother had. I was his priority, his mate. Losing me would likely make him want to end himself.

"OK. That's enough of that." Emmi moved around the kitchen like it was her own. "Dinner is ready."

And for the first time in days, I finally ate a proper meal.

After dinner, I was sitting on Orin's knee—we needed more chairs if we were going to host his entire family—when my head dropped with a *thud* against his shoulder. I hadn't realized that I'd started to fall asleep.

"All right." He stood, setting me on my feet. "I'm going to get my wife to bed. You're all free to stay here as long as you want and figure out your sleeping arrangements."

It wasn't late, but everything from the past few days had caught up to me. I wasn't as resilient as wolf shifters, I supposed. As for sleeping arrangements, Roman and Karina had been living in the house next door ,which Orin had bought when he'd bought this one. It was the only way to have privacy, he'd told me. Which meant his other brothers and parents could decide where they wanted to stay. Each house had three bedrooms. More than enough.

Usually, Daniel, Ivan, and their wives stayed at Roman's. Emmi and Anton would stay here. If Phillip were alive, he'd probably sleep at our house as well.

Right now, I couldn't play host to them. I was too tired.

Orin helped me up to the bedroom and closed the door behind us. Now, it was going to take everything for me to get undressed. "I'll help you," he said.

Nodding, I waited for him to make it over to me. As he touched me—innocent touches meant to help me into my nightclothes—that sleepiness slowly went away. Suddenly, I was filled with a need for something other than sleep.

Tomorrow could bring anything. Today was the day that we had and I wasn't going to face all of the bad without having all of the good.

"Orin," I whispered. He hadn't turned on any of the lights and only the moonlight streaming in through the curtains made sure we weren't in darkness. But I was naked. "I don't want to go right to sleep anymore."

A low growl rumbled in his chest as he stepped

closer to me, the heat of his body meaning I didn't need clothes. "What do you want?"

I settled my hands on his shoulders and lightly played with the hair on the back of his neck. "You," I said quietly. "Anything could happen tomorrow, right? I'd regret not using this time to be with you."

"You won't regret anything." He kissed me softly. "Because you'll be fine. Nothing is going to happen to you tomorrow. I promise you that."

My eyes and throat burned. That wasn't what I'd meant. "Can you make that same promise about yourself? Can you promise me nothing is going to happen to you?"

His jaw tightened because he knew he couldn't make that promise. He'd made it clear early on that he'd gladly lay down his life for mine and when it came to that, I had no doubt he'd do it. The Balodis had gotten their hands on me once and if that happened again, it'd only be because he was dead.

Orin's pack had a plan. I just hadn't been made aware of it, but whatever it was, I wouldn't like it. I didn't like any of this.

Orin wrapped his strong arms around me, his hands sliding down my backside. When he'd taken my clothes off, he'd taken everything. "I promise you'll be safe. That's the best I can do."

"How can you do this so easily?" A tear escaped and ran down my cheek. "How can you be so calm about what might happen?"

He used his hand to brush my hair away from my face, then his thumb raised it so I'd be looking up at him. "Easy, Elizabeth. It's to protect you. Compared to that, my life means nothing."

Tiny prickles of emotion ran a course through my body as more tears streamed down my face. "How can you say that?" I croaked out. "I'm not special, Orin." Then I rolled my eyes. "I guess my parentage makes me something, but I'm not more important."

"To me, you are." It sounded like the final words he wanted to say on the topic. "Now... on the bed. On your stomach."

A thrill ran through me, replacing anything else I might've been feeling right then. Or mostly replaced. While I got settled on my stomach, the sound of him getting naked filled the room, then his warmth was all around me. He ran his fingertips down my spine.

"You're the most beautiful creature I've ever seen." I heard him, but his voice was so low that I didn't trust myself to have made the words out. Then he kissed my back and worked his way down.

"Orin." It came out like a sigh. I wanted this.

Wanted him, but right this moment, I wanted to be able to see him.

As if he knew all of that simply from me saying his name, he said, "Flip over." And I did. Now he did the same thing to the front of me. He ran his fingers down my body, starting at my throat and not stopping until he was teasing between my legs, which I spread immediately.

Orin kissed me slowly, but fully. It was the most erotic kiss of my life until that point. It was all tongue and wetness and stealing my breath. "Orin," I said again because right now, it was the only word I knew. He'd barely touched me and I was on fire, ready to ignite the entire house. He pushed my legs apart and settled between them. The first lick made my eyes roll back in my head.

Nothing had prepared me for this moment, not even all of the other times with him. They had all been fantastic, but tonight... there was something different. It had to be the threat lingering over us that put more emotion than I'd known I'd possessed into this.

He kissed me and sucked my clitoris, bringing me right to the edge. As soon as my breath quickened, he thrust two fingers inside me, which shoved me off the best cliff of my life. My orgasm was so powerful that it left me breathless and feeling as if all of my muscles had gone away. Orin kissed down my thigh before hovering over me.

"Elizabeth," he said quietly, making me open my eyes. I ran my fingers down his cheek as he wet his lips. "I don't want to put a condom on, but I will if you want me to."

I furrowed my brows. He'd explained how condoms worked to me, something I would never have learned if he hadn't come along and he always wore one. Always. Since he was very thorough in his teaching, I knew his ejaculate was what would get me pregnant and we had decided not to chance it, given that we couldn't know if I would survive childbirth.

No one knew for sure, but with me, it seemed like more of a risk. But my aunt had children and she was fine. There wasn't any sense to be made of it.

"I—"

"I'll grab one," he said, but I grabbed his shoulders so he wouldn't move.

"I didn't say that. I'm just surprised. You were the one who didn't want to risk it."

"I know." He kissed my forehead. "I don't. I won't. I'll pull out, but I just want to feel you. You're not sure, though, so I'll get one. I don't want to do anything you don't want me to."

He went to move again, but as before, I stopped him. "I trust you, Orin. I'd want to have your baby, anyway. It wouldn't be a bad thing." But we'd ignore the whole *dying in childbirth* risk.

After lifting one of my legs, he pushed inside me.

It wasn't a full moon—the time that everything about him got bigger—but this was different. It was better. It was him and me. He moved slowly at first, then both of us were pushing for harder, faster... more.

Until his muscles tightened and he quickly pulled out of me, spreading his semen across my stomach. "Don't move." He sounded as winded as I felt when he left and returned with a wet cloth to clean up the mess he'd made.

Then we were back in bed and there wasn't anything in this world that could've kept me awake.

In the morning, I woke to pounding on the bedroom door. Orin jumped out of bed and opened the door only enough to talk to the person outside without exposing me to whoever it was. Based on his footsteps, I thought it was Roman.

"What?" Orin snapped.

"Whoa, brother. I don't want to be at your door

any more than you want me here, but we've got problems." That was Roman. He'd always been the most comfortable with me, so it made sense that he was the one usually sent to us.

"What kind of problems?"

"Part of the pack didn't make it to town."

I flung myself up, holding the sheet to my chest. If that meant what I thought it did...

"What do you mean?"

"There was an attack. We've lost four members and four others aren't in the best shape."

Orin's dark eyes slid over to me. They were darker than normal, as if a storm was brewing inside of him.

No. It was a storm he was going to unleash.

That was the look he had when he was out for blood.

Chapter Eighteen

"WHAT HAPPENED?" Orin asked urgently and we got to the kitchen.

There were papers spread out on the table and breakfast on the counter. Karina was still scrambling eggs as we walked in.

"We're not sure," his father told him. Orin went toward the guys while I slid over near the stove. Their voices moved to the background.

"It's bad," I said and it wasn't a question.

"Yes," she whispered back.

I shook my head. "This is why I don't want your pack to fight to protect me." I shifted my weight from one foot to another since I had nothing else to do with the nervous energy.

"They're your pack, too, Elizabeth," she said,

though she didn't indicate that she thought I was wrong.

"I know. That's why I don't want anyone hurt." I sighed. "Orin needs to let them have me or... I don't know. We'll leave. Never come back."

She turned to me like I'd just said the dumbest thing anyone could think of. "You can't take a wolf from his pack." Then she rolled her eyes. "I guess you can, but it will hurt him. Like a hundred tiny knives on fire poking through him. Breaking from your pack is not something you do."

But my mother and Audrey had done it. Did that hurt them? Was it painful? "I don't want anyone else hurt, Karina."

"Neither do I, but this... this is our life. This is what we do."

"We need some place to take the wounded," Anton said over the others. "We've sent some men to bring them here, but your house isn't big enough for your mother and Karina to nurse them."

I raised an eyebrow at Karina. Apparently, she and Emmi wouldn't be fighting, either. A little bit of pressure was released from my chest knowing that those two should be fine.

"We'll make due," Emmi told him, but her husband was already shaking his head.

"No. They'll find you all here. That defeats the purpose of everything we're doing right now."

Then it hit me. I had a place large enough for them to convalesce along with anyone else. A place with bad memories that could now be of use.

"I know somewhere," I said, but no one paid any attention to me. "I said I have someplace," I called out louder, bringing their attention to me.

"Where's that?" Anton asked.

"My father's house. It's large. Many rooms. Plenty of room, actually."

Ivan walked out from behind the table. "We've been there. It would work and no one would likely look there for injured werewolves."

"The staff," Orin added. "We'd have to get rid of them."

Nodding, I said, "I can do that. I'll have them get the rooms ready and then leave."

Orin came to a stop in front of me. "Are you sure?"

My lips parted to assure him that it was fine when Ivan slid in beside him with his arms over his chest. "Stop treating her like she can't handle anything, Orin."

My lips parted in surprise. Ivan hadn't said a

kind word to me ever, I didn't think, yet here he was on my side?

"Stay out of it, Ivan," Orin countered. "There are things you don't know."

"Doesn't matter." He brushed a hand through the air as if to brush Orin away with it. "The shit that's happening... She's still standing, so if she says she's going to do something, she'll do it."

No one knew me better than Orin and I knew that he was just trying to protect me, but it felt good to have someone else on my side, at least about this one thing. Sure, Karina had been, but this was one of Orin's brothers. Somehow, it meant something different.

Orin eyed me then finally nodded. "All right. I'll take you."

"We'll take her." Emmi raised an eyebrow at her son. "Unless you don't think I can take care of her."

Orin sighed and held his hands up in defeat. "I didn't say that."

Emmi might've looked a little older, because she was, but she wasn't old and the way she carried herself said that she could rip the throat out of anyone who *thought* about hurting one of her kids.

Now, I was one of her kids.

Before I got out the door with Emmi and Karina,

Orin pulled me aside. "We'll meet you all there in a little while. We have some things to figure out first, but it will be before the injured show up."

"I'm just happy there's something that I can do here."

"Yeah." He didn't sound all that excited, but he leaned down to kiss me, anyway. Then I was on my way to a house I had vowed to never step foot in again.

The three of us rode in silence, outside of me telling Emmi where to turn. Orin had started to teach me to drive, but I still wasn't the most comfortable with it. I hadn't had the time to practice much and thought that comfort would come with more practice.

We stepped out of the car once Emmi had brought it to a stop and Karina removed her stylish sunglasses. "This is where you grew up?"

Nodding, I told her, "It is."

"How magical." She shut the door on the car.

"Not magical at all." I wouldn't go into any details.

This time, I didn't knock when entering, but Mrs. Atherton was hurrying across the entryway to greet us.

"Elizabeth." She stretched out her arms to hug

me while eyeing my company suspiciously. "I wasn't expecting you."

"I know, Mrs. Atherton." She'd been the only warm smile in the house my entire childhood. "This is Orin's mother, and his sister-in-law, Karina."

"Welcome, Mrs. Vilkatas." She greeted Emmi then gave Karina a nod.

"Please, call me 'Emmi.'"

"Is there something I can do for you, Elizabeth?" she asked me. "Is there something you're looking for? Would you like chef to make up some lunch?"

"No, thank you." I moved farther into the house. "This is going to be an odd request, but could you and the maids prepare all of the bedrooms with fresh linen?"

"We did that yesterday, but we can change everything out."

"Oh, no." I held up a hand to stop her from leaving us so she could give the orders. "If you did it yesterday, that's fine." One day wouldn't result in dusty sheets and I knew they rotated the sheets in every room regularly. I just didn't know how regularly. "Could you air out the rooms a bit? Just crack the windows. We'll shut them."

"Of course." Again, she eyed the women I'd brought with me. "Will you be having company?"

"Yes," I told her because we would be. "Also, could you have one of the maids bring all of the medical aid kits to the dayroom?"

She furrowed her brows. "Elizabeth… is everything all right?"

"It is." I gave her a reassuring smile and squeezed her arm. "But after that, I'd like you to give the entire staff a holiday."

"What?" The surprise in her voice was genuine because they'd never gotten a holiday as far back as I could remember. Each had a single day off every week, something I would change if I was the one inheriting this house. One day off a week didn't seem like enough to me.

"Tell them all to go somewhere. Visit family. It doesn't matter where. Use the house account if they need it, but I need everyone to leave here for a little while."

"We're being fired?"

"No." I grabbed both of her arms. "No one is being let go. I just need the house empty for a little while. Get information for everyone and make sure I have yours. I'll contact you when it's safe to come back, then you can contact them. I intend to keep this house much like it is if my father left it to me. There will be some changes, but only for the better."

The staff had been loyal to my father and that should be rewarded. Mrs. Atherton might've been the only one warm to me, but the rest were pleasant enough and their fear of my father had kept them at a distance. I wouldn't put any of them out into the cold. Probably most of this should've been handled by the butler, but Mrs. Atherton was the one I had a relationship with.

If I had my way, she'd be running the entire house, putting her over the butler. Sure, that was unheard of by like with everything else in my life, I meant to mix the old that I liked with the new that I desired. After all, no one would complain to keep their jobs.

"'Safe'? Elizabeth, is everything all right?"

I offered her what I hoped was a reassuring smile. After all, I didn't know if everything was all right.

"Yes," I told her. "Some members of Orin's family had an accident and I thought this would be somewhere they could recuperate. It won't take long..." I glanced back at Emmi. The werewolves healed quicker, but I didn't know how badly any of them had been hurt.

"A few days," she said. "Maybe a week."

"See? I just think it'd be easier for them if the house were a little quieter."

Mrs. Atherton nodded, but I could see she was still trying to figure this out. "I will get them organized and they will be out within two hours."

"Perfect. Thank you, Mrs. Atherton."

She scurried off to take care of the things I'd asked for and knowing her my entire life meant that I could have confidence that when she said they'd all be gone in two hours, they'd all be gone in two hours.

"What do we need to do?" I asked.

"We'll go through supplies and make a list of things we need. Karina can fetch those from the pharmacist."

So that's what we did. Once the medical kits had begun arriving, we were able to access everything, though I had no idea what we were even looking for. These wolves healed quickly, but my experience with Phillip was that they could bleed to death before the healing kicked in.

Karina did have to get things from the pharmacist and while she was gone, I showed Emmi the house. The maids worked quickly, avoiding us at every turn.

Then we were ready. Mrs. Atherton and Chef were the last to leave the house. I didn't need to know the details. Just that they were gone. She did tell me before she left that my father's lawyer had dropped off a large envelope for me. I thanked her, but I wouldn't be looking at it anytime soon.

It was good timing, too, because the rest of the Vilkatas men showed up then. Not long after that, the injured came and it was a bustle of activity to get them settled. There were so many pack members here, I'd never learn all of their names, that much was certain.

We were barely done when Daniel burst through the front door. "They're on their way."

"All right, pack." Anton's voice bellowed through the entryway. "It's time." And they all looked ready.

However, as the pack filed out of my house, Emmi and Karina stayed back to take care of the injured parties. But Orin also didn't leave.

"What are you doing?" I asked him.

"Staying here."

"What?" This was me in between a rock and a hard place. I didn't want Orin to go and be in danger. Not even for a second. But I knew that it'd kill him to stay back. "Why? Is it me? I can take care of myself." Then I shrugged. "Probably."

"It's not just you, Elizabeth," he countered. "It's the injured. It's my mother. It's Karina. We know they know about this place, though we doubt they'll think we're here. Your essence was gone long before they came here." That was right. I'd forgotten that the wolves would've been able to smell me, but I hadn't been inside this house since I'd given my father my mother's journal back. I made a mental note to search everything to find out if she had more. "You go help my mom. I'm going to check outside."

Orin was our sentry meant to keep everyone in the house safe, but I knew that he would've much rather be out fighting with his pack. On one hand, I was grateful. On the other... no. I was just going to be grateful.

Emmi, Karina, and I got all of the men taken care of. They'd heal soon, the signs of which were already showing up. It was all about keeping them from bleeding to death before it happened and Karina said it'd take them a day—two for the more severely injured—to get their full strength back.

"This would make a good packhouse," Karina said when the three of us were walking back downstairs. I'd chosen to wear trousers today, as had both of the other women, and no heels. Heels were a hindrance if something happened and we had to run.

"Isn't the packhouse up north?" I asked.

She shrugged. "We could move. The weather is more tolerable down here."

I didn't think all of the families would want to move, but I also wasn't up to date on all the pack rules. If the alpha—Anton—moved, did the rest of them have to? Could they have two packhouses? The entire pack didn't live in the packhouse, so where would they live if they moved here? Maybe buy houses in town.

Plus, I'd have to talk to Orin and his parents about the staff here. Could they really stay if werewolves were going to be living here? Orin alone, sure but all of them? I didn't think so.

All of that was for later.

"Hey." Karina pulled me to a stop. "Did you happen to touch any of the men today?"

I furrowed my brows. "What kind of woman do you think I am?" I asked, hoping the humor would come through.

She snorted. "Elizabeth, you know what I mean. We should've had you check all the men for the mark of death."

I shook my head at her description. That wasn't what I wanted to be known for. "I did," I admitted. I hadn't told anyone I was doing it and most of it had been just a simple brush as I'd passed them. It'd been crowded enough that no one had noticed. "I didn't see anything." She grinned at me widely. "That doesn't mean nothing bad is going to happen, Karina. It's just they aren't going to die in the very near future. There are variables I can't control."

"I know. But this makes me feel a little better."

Which was funny because she hadn't acted like she was worried at all.

"Wait." I stopped and listened more carefully. "Do you hear that?"

It took Karina and Emmi three seconds to focus their hearing, then their eyes widened.

"Orin." Emmi took off in a run.

Karina and I chased after her, though I was the slowest of the three. We were out the front door, down the steps, and then racing toward the side of the house. When we got there, my steps faltered.

Orin was barely on his feet. He staggered and fell into a man. That wasn't like him. He was the strongest man I knew.

"What's wrong with him?" I asked without taking my eyes off my husband.

Karina looked at Emmi. "Wolfsbane?"

Emmi shook her head. "That would've affected them too. I don't know. But I'm not losing another son."

Then right before my eyes, Emmi grew larger and her skin prickled with new hair as everything about her changed until she was no longer human. Her wolf had light hair, maybe a sign of the gray I'd noticed poking around the edges near her ears. Then the wolf was running.

Karina turned to me and held my arms tightly. "I have to help her," she said, already sounding out of breath. "Anton will know she shifted. They'll head this way."

"How will he know?" A fight was breaking out and this probably wasn't the time to ask.

"It's the mate bond. We know when the other shifts. Just stay back, Elizabeth." Because she'd know better than to tell me to go back to the house.

Then Karina morphed into the same animal as my mother-in-law. She was running at the three men who had Orin.

Why hadn't Orin shifted? Why hadn't the men?

That would have to wait. Right now, I was going to try to help. My father had given me extra power and I was going to use it. Somehow. Without getting hurt, though at this point, I only cared because Orin did.

I ran toward the melee.

The sound of snarls and growls filled the air as

the men who'd had Orin shifted, which caused them to drop him to the ground. I moved my focus and ran for him.

"Orin!" I called out when I dropped to my knees beside him. "Orin." I pulled on him. He was too heavy for me to move, but he was alive, that much was sure. And relief washed over me when no flash of his death came.

Finally, I got him to his feet, but most of his weight was on me, making it difficult to get him away. Then he groaned and pushed me away, but there wasn't much effort behind it. He was weak.

One of the wolves pounced on him, but given the fact that there were five werewolves in a small area, I didn't know which one it was.

"Orin!" I called as he fell to the ground and a wolf's nails sunk into his arm.

That was it. I was sucking all of the energy out of this thing. I charged, but right before I got to Orin, another wolf slammed him to the ground and three more wolves ran at full speed to join the fight. This had to be Orin's dad and brothers. Which meant I could focus on Orin.

Again, right as my hand touched his, someone grabbed me. But this time, it wasn't before I was hit with a vision.

Orin was on a chair with a drooling beast before him. The beast paced, then Orin said something and the beast grabbed him by the throat, ripping him apart.

I gasped. Then a sob came out, my chest heavy as if something was sitting on it and my knees gave out.

No, no, no, no. This couldn't be happening and why was someone dragging me away?

"Stop fighting me." That was Roman's human voice. "I need to get you out of here."

"No. Roman. I can help. I saw it. Orin's going to die. I need to help!" My voice didn't sound like my own and all of the words were coming out at once.

The fight continued, but I got farther and farther away as my naked brother-in-law was pulling me away and I screamed my husband's name.

Chapter Nineteen

ROMAN THREW me roughly through the door, then closed it behind him and stood in front of it, like he was a guard intent on not letting me out of this house. He was naked with his arms over his chest.

"What are you doing?" I screamed. "I can help. Let me help."

"This was the plan, Elizabeth," he snapped. "If anything happened, I had to get you to safety."

Rivulets of tears streamed down my face. "Why?" I demanded. "I could suck their energy. I could—"

"This is what Orin wanted," he yelled, which was the reminder that he'd just left his family, including his wife, out there fighting, but he was standing here because of me. "Do you think I want to be in here instead of out there? He made me promise."

He'd promised to keep me safe. If I kept pushing, it'd keep Roman here instead of where he could be helping his family and making sure my husband was all right.

"Go," I told him more calmly, but the tears weren't stopping. I wasn't crying exactly yet the tears still fell. "Go help them, Roman. I'll stay here." He cocked his head to the side. "I promise," I whispered.

"I can't chance it."

"I'll go upstairs to one of the men's rooms. I'll check on them. One is almost healed. He can keep me there."

Roman stalked toward me and I realized again that he was totally naked. "Swear you'll stay there, Elizabeth."

"I swear. Go."

He was out the door so quickly that I didn't have the chance to see if he was going to die. Since I couldn't worry about that now, I ran upstairs to the first room with the least injured wolf shifter inside. He was sitting up in bed with a serious look on his face.

"What're you doing here?" he asked. I hadn't learned their names yet, but they all knew who I was.

"I promised Roman that I'd stay in this room until the fight outside is over."

"I'm listening to it now."

Right! I could be listening to see what was going on. This *enhanced senses* thing was going to take some getting used to. I dropped myself into a chair and focused.

"Why here?" he asked before I got very far.

"I told him you're the least injured and could keep me by force if necessary."

"Is that what I'm supposed to do?"

I nodded. There was no sense trying to hide it. He didn't have a shirt on and his golden skin almost sparkled in the sunlight. How the neighbors weren't hearing the fighting, I didn't know. They wouldn't see it because of the landscaping that my father had put in and our closest neighbor wasn't right next door. It wasn't like in the city, but still, these sounds traveled.

So I focused and tried to hear everything. All I got were loud snarks and growls and the snapping of jaws. I couldn't tell who anyone was or who was winning, but slowly, all the noise faded away, so I looked up at the man who was both my current captor and protector.

"Then come in," he told me, but instead, I

hopped to my feet and raced out of the room, down the stairs.

The door burst open.

First Anton and Daniel came through, carrying Ivan. All back in human form and all completely naked. This was why Orin had said there were no hang-ups about sex and nudity in the pack.

"Is he all right?" I asked.

"Clearly not," Daniel snapped.

"I'm fine," Ivan countered. "That fucker came out of nowhere."

Emmi quickly put on a dressing gown and ordered them to take her son into the dayroom. Karina came in next, so I brought her a gown of her own. Clothes weren't the most important thing, but I wanted to do something.

Roman entered last and shut the door behind him.

But where in the hell was my husband?

"Roman?" I asked, my voice cracking at the word.

He came over to me. "They dragged him away. More showed up, even though the packs were fighting deep into the woods."

"Why was he so weak?" I asked.

"We don't know. We need to get Ivan fixed up and then we'll figure it out."

"Roman." I grabbed his arm to stop him from going into that room. When no image of his death hit me, my shoulders released. "I saw him die," I whispered.

"We're not going to let that happen." He walked away to check on his brother.

I didn't have the strength to ask, *What if it's already happened?*

It took me several minutes to compose myself enough to go into that room. All I could think about was Orin and the fact that he might be dead right this minute.

After blowing out a breath to calm the rising panic, I walked inside.

Ivan had a blanket thrown over his lower half and the rest of the men had put trousers on, though at this point, I didn't care.

"How is he?" I asked.

"I'm fine," Ivan said, but clearly, he was in pain.

"Touch him," Emmi demanded. She wanted to see if he was going to die, which meant his injury was more severe than he was letting on.

I pushed past Roman and Daniel then grabbed

Ivan's hand and concentrated. Nothing happened, so I stepped back.

"I didn't see anything."

The tension released from Emmi's shoulders and Anton grunted his appreciation.

"Now," I said, smoothing my hands over my clothes. "What about Orin? I saw him die."

Anton loomed over me like a big, scary... werewolf in human form, I guess. "When does it happen?"

"I don't know," I told him. "It doesn't work like that. It has to be soon because I don't see people dying from old age."

"That means we have to go now." Ivan was pushing himself up off the sofa until his mother pushed him back down. She wasn't that gentle about it.

"Stay down." Her tone meant that not a single person would argue with her.

"We'll go," Anton agreed. "But we need to think about this. They don't want Orin. They want her, so I think he'll be safe for at least a little while. Killing him would mean they have no chance at her. They'll want to use him for leverage." Then he focused back on me. "Did you see who kills him?"

I shook my head. "It was a werewolf shifted, but I can't tell most of you apart."

He nodded slowly as I spoke. "All right."

I snapped my head to the side. Someone was outside the front door. I turned and hurried that way, yanking it open before anyone caught up to me, but I could feel the weight of the Vilkatas family at my back.

Daniel reached forward and grabbed the man standing on the doorstep, yanked him through, then threw him against the wall with his massive arm over the man's throat.

"I'm just the messenger," the man got out. "I have a message from the Balodis."

"He's a shifter," Roman said, as if any of us had doubted it.

Daniel released the pressure against the man's neck, but only enough so that he could speak. "What do they want?" Though we all already knew.

He raised an arm and pointed a finger at me. "Her. Alpha says that if we don't have her by nightfall, the werewolf dies."

Which means that I saw Orin's death a number of hours in advance. I wished the visions came with a sense of time, but that also meant that he was still alive right now.

Daniel pressed harder against the man's neck.

The man quietly said, "And if I don't come back unharmed, he dies now."

"Daniel," I begged. "Please... don't."

It wasn't hard to see that Daniel wanted to kill the man. Hell, *I* wanted to kill the man for being part of what had taken Orin from us. But that wasn't going to help.

Daniel released him but still loomed over him so he didn't try to come farther into the house. It'd be a stupid move, given that he was sorely outnumbered.

"Give us your message."

"The alpha wants her by nightfall or your pack member dies. They know what she is and aren't going to stop until they have her." The way he spoke sounded as if he didn't agree with all of this and since I didn't understand the inner politics of wolf packs, I couldn't be sure.

"Is that all?" Daniel demanded. The man nodded. "Then get out." He didn't turn away from the door until we were sure the man was gone.

"What're we going to do?" Karina asked.

"Come back in here," Ivan called out. "Or I'm coming out there."

Emmi sighed but led the group of us back to the dayroom so that Ivan could be part of the conversation. He was already looking better. Some of his color had come back and the bleeding had definitely slowed.

When we were all inside, Emmi sat near Ivan's feet on the sofa while Anton dropped into the chair near his head. Karina sat in the chair across from them with Roman leaning on the arm. Daniel and I, however, made no move to sit. I didn't know if it was the same for him, but I couldn't sit. I had too many emotions running through me right now.

"So what're we going to do?" Karina asked. "Attack?"

"I furrowed my brows. "Where's the rest of the pack?"

"On their way back," Anton told me and I supposed since he was the alpha, he'd know. "We didn't suffer any losses. A few injuries that will heal quickly."

OK. This wolf sense or whatever they had to communicate with each other was something I wanted to have explained eventually, but right now, I needed to know about Orin.

"I'll go," I told them, causing Daniel to stop pacing.

"No," Roman said immediately.

"What else is there to do?" I asked, louder than

necessary. "They want me. If we give them me, they'll stop fighting you. Both sides win."

"*You* lose!" Roman roared. "*Orin* loses."

"Yes." The fear started to creep up my neck, making me swallow down the bitter taste that had risen in my throat. "But all of you would be safe. Orin would be safe."

"You wouldn't be," Karina said quietly. "You wouldn't be safe, Elizabeth."

"I would be. They're not going to kill me if they want to... breed with me." It made it sound so nasty, yet I was reminded of last night when Orin hadn't used the condom and the fact that we could've made a baby if he hadn't withdrawn at the last moment.

Roman's eyes darkened. "There are a lot of ways to hurt you without killing you, Elizabeth."

My stomach roiled and I felt like I was going to throw up. It was the same feeling I'd had when I'd contracted influenza as a child. The coughing had made me throw up again and again.

"Are we all forgetting that I can drain power? Maybe we can figure something out so that I can drain them and give you an advantage. I don't know." I blew out a desperate breath. "But what I do know is that if we don't do what they say, Orin dies. If he dies, I won't want to live, anyway."

Roman looked over at his father, who sat in his chair, running his index finger over his bottom lip like he was considering everything I'd said. Then Roman groaned.

"Orin will kill every one of us if we let this happen." There was a warning in Roman's voice and I believed every word. However...

"He'd have to be alive to kill you," I reminded him. "Before Orin and I left my father... my real father, he gave me a power boost." I held up a hand. "Don't ask me how it works because I don't understand any of this."

"Wait." Daniel snapped his fingers. "That shit that was here said they know what she is. So they know about the banshee, but they must also know about the incubus. I'd bet that they think that's the secret to breed without the woman dying."

"Why does it matter?" I asked.

"Because they'll pass you around, Elizabeth," Roman said darkly, instilling a new fear in me.

Before I'd thought they just wanted me to breed with a single member, but the idea of multiple men... A shiver ran down my spine. Roman narrowed his eyes.

"That *should* scare you," he said menacingly. This was a side of him that I hadn't seen before.

"They'll pass you around from man to man so that you can pop out a baby every ten months. Again and again, until you're worn out and you simply die. That's if you survive the first one. You won't be a person to them and you won't see those babies, either. They have women who will raise them, I bet. Women who'd give anything to have a baby and not die in childbirth."

Tears burned my eyes and throat, but I wasn't going to crack. All of that made me sick and scared the hell out of me, but if it was what I had to do to save Orin, I'd do it. My life wasn't more important than his.

Anton's jaw was granite and his eyes hard. "Are you sure about this?"

"Yes." My answer was immediate and clear. I'd do anything to save Orin.

"All right." He pushed up out of his chair.

Karina gasped and Emmi said, "Anton, no. I told him I'd protect her."

"We'll come up with a plan. If she can drain their energy, we can overwhelm them. I don't know where their power boost is coming from, Emija. It's the only thing we can do."

They weren't sending me out to be used up by the Balodis pack. Anton was bringing me in as someone who might be able to help. Now, the threat of the former happening loomed over me, but if everything went to plan, I'd be back here with my husband soon.

If not... I'd accept my choice.

"Orin's going to kill us all." Roman said it to everyone, but his eyes were burning my skin.

If I lived through this, my husband was going to be angrier than I'd ever seen him.

Chapter Twenty

Daniel left as soon as the decision was made to see if he could locate Orin and if the possibility of a rescue was there so that they wouldn't turn me over.

Personally, I didn't think Daniel cared if I was gone. After all, I'd brought a lot of chaos to their family even before I'd known anything about them. However, he loved his brother, and I was reminded of their unspoken vow to protect each other's families. I was Orin's family.

This was the entire reason why I was willing to sacrifice myself. I couldn't be the end to the Vilkatas pack and the Balodis had something going on to make them so strong right now.

"Elizabeth." Roman was right outside of my bedroom door, the bedroom I'd grown up in. I'd come up here to have a moment to myself. To have just a small slip of time where things were slightly normal. Or at least could feel normal.

I pushed to my feet. "Did something happen? Is Daniel back?"

He shook his head, so I sat slowly back down on my bed. Orin had been the only man to ever be in here, yet I didn't feel awkward now that Roman was.

"I've just come to talk to you," he told me. His hair was a mess. Everyone's was after the day we'd already had. By the end of the night, the pack would be able to heal.

"How's Ivan?"

"Healed." I'd figured as much. "You can't do this, Elizabeth."

I didn't need him to elaborate on what he was talking about. "I have to. They'll kill him, Roman. I saw it. Somehow, I saw further ahead, but I saw it nonetheless. They'll kill him. They won't kill me."

He growled in his chest. "There are worse things than death, Elizabeth."

I assumed he meant the breeding. Did I want to do it? No. But it was worth Orin's life. "I know that," I snapped. "I know there are, but right now... It's all we have. Maybe you all will figure out how to get me back. I don't know."

"Once you're pregnant, they're not going to let you out of their sight. Getting you back is going to be nearly impossible."

"But Orin won't be killed." That was my singular focus right now and I finally understood fully what Orin had felt when the Balodis had gotten me the first time and why Phillip had laid down his life to give me back to his brother.

"He'll be dead, anyway!" He screamed, making me jump. "Don't you see that? If you're gone, he's going to be dead, anyway."

"Metaphorically."

"Literally," he yelled, though at a much lower level. "He's not going to want to live without you, which means he's going to do some really dangerous shit to get you back and it'll kill him. That's *if* you're not killed and the feeling of ten thousand knives stabbing him doesn't drive him insane first."

They'd told me when one of them lost their mate, it felt that way. Like a death from ten thousand tiny cuts. It was their version of the most intense grief a person could feel. Diana was coming out the other side of it, but if one of them was in it without the support of the pack, it went a very different way.

I didn't want that for Orin, but he'd survive because he would have that support.

Did I understand it all? No. But just because I wouldn't feel the way they would didn't mean I was willing to grieve my husband when there was something I could have done about it.

"Roman, my dad, Coltar, gave me extra power. I just haven't been able to tap into it yet and I don't know what it'll do. But if I can, when I'm in with them, maybe I can weaken then and all of you can come get me. I don't know, but I can't sit here like a fucking damsel in distress with all of you making sacrifices for me while I make none."

Humor played at his lips.

My jaw tightened. "Why are you trying not to smile right now?"

"You said, 'fucking,'" he admitted. "I don't think you've ever cursed in front of me."

"In front of *anyone*." I threw my hands in the air and let them slap against my legs on the way down. "I'm done caring. I love your brother. He's saved me more times than I can count and it's my turn to save him."

"He knows what you're doing," he admitted.

I jumped to my feet and ran over, pushing against his chest. "What do you mean? He can't know. He's there."

"It's the pack bond, Elizabeth. I know Orin's mentioned it but didn't go into detail about how it works for this very reason. First, it's really difficult to put words to it, but we can kind of send each other thoughts. It's how he'd call to me when we were at your aunt's. I didn't show up at her doorstep on accident."

"Someone told him about my plan this way?"

"*I* told him that way."

My lips parted in surprise. Roman had never been on board with this plan. I didn't think any of them really were, but most understood it was the only way and they were willing to let me go and to deal with Orin's wrath later.

Shaking my head, I took a step away from him. "I can't believe you told him. Roman, he could do something to hurry things up. To make them kill him before I have the chance to turn myself over."

"I know." He was set that I wasn't to do this. That Orin's wishes for me to be safe were more important than what I was willing to do.

Angry and sad tears burned my eyes as I took small steps away from him. "If he's already dead, Roman, I'll never forgive you." Then I turned my back to him, wrapped my arms around my middle, and let the tears fall.

"He's not dead yet," Roman whispered. "I don't think he's dead yet."

"Would you know? Would you feel it?"

"No."

"Then you can't know." I was set on not saying another word to him as long as I was here.

Daniel came back and said he didn't see an easy way to get to Orin. They could do it, but they would suffer big losses. It could decimate the pack. He'd seen some witch talisman around the compound, which complicated things.

This was the first mention of witches that I'd heard, or that I remembered, yet I wasn't shocked or surprised. In a world where there were werewolves, banshees, and incubi, why wouldn't there have been witches? Real witches.

"One of them must be tapping into something big," Emmi offered. "I don't know this area as well, but if there was a location that saw witch tragedy… that could be it."

"How?" I asked.

Emmi looked over as if she'd just realized I was there. "If a witch dies through trauma or from serious tragedy, their powers will sometimes be left."

"Like a witch's essence," Ivan added.

"Right, and a decently powerful witch could tap

into that." She glanced at her husband. "If they made their packhouse at that location and then found a witch to syphon the power... they're going to be unstoppable."

"We're going to stop them," Anton countered. "Just not on their property." He moved over to the center of the group. "I think we're going to go there, lure them out, and try to wipe them out. Even if we get Orin back, we can't just go back home and leave them to run free. Especially if they're using witches to do their bidding now." He took a breath, then turned to me. "That is if Elizabeth is still willing to be the bait."

Roman's growl was the only thing to break the silence until I said, "Of course I am. I'll do anything to get Orin out of there."

Anton nodded once. "Good. Because we're going to have to let them have you."

"No." Roman's response was immediate.

My eyes narrowed on my father-in-law. "That was the plan all along."

"Right. But we need Orin. Which means we're going to have to get him back here and heal him before we can act. They're probably using silver on him in some way." When I furrowed my brows, he said, "Silver is something we either can't heal from if, say, we're hit from a silver bullet, or that takes us longer to heal from if, say, we are stabbed with a silver blade."

Roman growled again, which I'd learned they sometimes couldn't help. "You're saying we're going to let them take her, get him back here to heal, and *then* go after her? They could get her pregnant in that amount of time."

"I don't care," I said loudly.

"*Orin* will care," he yelled back.

There wasn't a large gap between us, but I still closed it and looked up at him. I was the smallest person in the room, but Orin had helped me find my backbone and I wasn't about to lose it now. "If I come back pregnant and Orin doesn't want me, I'll have to live with that. But I saw him die once. I'm not doing it again."

"It's not about *him* not wanting *you!*" Roman's roar made me flinch. "He'll always want you no matter what. It's about us letting you go through this."

"It's settled," Anton barked, the sound letting us know that all discussion and planning were done.

It was decided.

As the sun began to drop in the sky, we headed out into the woods to the location where the Balodis had said they wanted to make the trade. It was closer to their packhouse than to ours and that was probably for a reason. I didn't know how long we'd walked but once we were there, we were alone, for a short while. The rest of the Vilkatas pack were just into the tree line, ready to shift and fight. We had to assume the same with the Balodis pack when one man led the way out of the trees with two behind them carrying Orin, one on each side.

He was hurt. He didn't look alive, but Anton would confirm that before anything else happened. There was blood trickling down the side of his face as well as staining his clothes. I slapped a hand over my mouth to keep from sobbing and it took all of my willpower to not run over to him.

"Is my son alive?" Anton asked from several feet in front of us. He and the leader of the Balodis were standing almost toe to toe.

Their leader was large, but Anton was larger both in height and width. Realistically, that didn't matter as much. The Balodis leader was a tall man with a stocky build and dark hair that I wasn't sure he'd washed recently.

"He is... How long he stays that way, well, no one knows." A sly grin spread across his face and if *I* was having a hard time not scratching the man's eyes out, then Orin's family must've really been exercising self-control. "So we're trading what's yours for what's mine, correct?" Anton nodded once. "Perfect. Because she was always a member of this pack. It doesn't matter what her whore mother did. Elizabeth belongs to us."

My stomach turned at him characterizing my mother that way, but I kept my mouth shut.

"No!" Roman yelled as he began to run for me. Ivan and Daniel caught him and pulled him away as he continued fighting them.

"We need to get this done before your son ruins it," the man said.

Anton didn't turn to look at me when he said, "Elizabeth."

I stepped forward and didn't stop until I was next to him, which led the Balodis to bring Orin out. Swallowing down the acid that rose in my throat when I saw him, I tried to keep my body from vibrating.

Orin was barely able to walk on his own. His face was dirty and marred with blood—his I would suspect. His strong muscles hung loose and I could only imagine what they'd done to him.

As soon as he was close enough, I touched the

side of his face and closed my eyes. Orin leaned into my touch.

No vision came. If we stayed on this track, Orin would be safe.

A quick glance at Emmi let her know that he'd be all right.

Then it was time to trade.

One of the Balodis gripped my upper arm as Emmi and Karina came forward to take Orin. He groaned at the movement, but they propped him on their strong shoulders to start moving... and then something else happened.

The trees rustled when there was no wind.

"Tell your pack not to attack," the Balodis man urged.

"That's not mine," Anton countered. "We're ready for yours if they don't stand down."

"It's not mine."

We were all looking at the area of movement, but there was nothing there.

Until Coltar came into focus. He hadn't been there and now he was, though I had no way of knowing how. Then, three other men—younger than Coltar and looking far too similar to him to not be the brothers I'd never met—then Meredith and another woman who was the spitting image of Meredith. It had to be her mother.

"I believe you're making a deal for my daughter," Coltar said as the entire group of them walked toward us and he was looking directly at the Balodis leader.

"*Your* daughter?"

Coltar glanced to where the man was holding on to me and tightening his grip. "I'll thank you to let her go."

The man jerked me toward him.

Coltar gave him an evil grin. "You're really going to regret doing that."

And then all hell broke loose.

The trilogy comes to an end.

After everything Orin and Elizabeth have been through, it's time to put an end to the constant threat to her life.

She now has a father who cares if she lives or dies, a husband who will trade his life for her own, and a family like she's never had before.

No one is getting through all of them to get to her.

That doesn't mean they won't try.

PREORDER MOONKISSED

**After living under my father's rule, I'm
about to break free.**

My father has kept me on a short leash my entire life.

The Orin comes for me.

Finding out what he is... scares the hell out of me.

Finding out I'm his supposed mate... I don't know
that I'll recover.

START READING MOONSTRUCK TODAY

Being the daughter of my people's leaders, I should understand protocol and appropriate behavior. Problem is, I understand both, I just don't follow them.

But I have a different plan.

There's a boy... now a man, who is supposed to be powerful. I want him on our side.

What I didn't know is that together, he and I might be unstoppable.

Now I just have to find him.

START READING THE GREMLIN PRINCE TODAY

I'm a witch. Or so they tell me.

Finding out I'm a witch isn't even the weirdest part of my day. Having the guy who hated me in high school stand before me to tell me that I am, is.

Somehow, I'm supposed to learn spells and how to ground myself to the elements, fight the fact that I want him like I want air, and not freak out that my parents are part of a shadow coven trying to pull me over to the dark side.

Yeah. No problem.

START READING CURSED MAGIC TODAY

He was my brother's best friend and off limits.

The world knows Silas Briggs as the baseball heartthrob on a hot streak. I know him as brother's former friend and my teenage crush.
Four years ago, he broke my young heart by making me think there could be something between us.

Then he left town and never looked back.

Now I'm back and working for the team, hoping that we can be friendly. Then I see him in person and friendship is the last thing on my mind.

START READING KISSING THE PLAYER TODAY

Do you love rock stars?

FOREVER GRAYSON

Forever 18 Book 1

One night three years ago is coming back to haunt me.

It was supposed to be one night then I'd never see him again. One night at a dive bar where I met someone who could scratch an itch.

He wasn't famous then.

Now he's a rock star.

A rock star whose manager just hired me to be the band's stylist. It's a dream job to me but it could be a nightmare.
Is it worse if he remembers me? Or worse if he doesn't?

START READING FOREVER GRAYSON NOW

Love your rock stars? Check out…
Daisy *Pushing Daisies Book 1*

Is it weird that I'm in a band with my brothers?
Not to me.

When I'm moved off our bus and onto the one that belongs to the hot manager of the headlining band, I know something's wrong.

Lawson is willing to take me on so some crazy fan can't get to me but when things heat up… he backs off. Says he's too old for me.

It's a small age gap. It doesn't mean a thing.

START READING DAISY NOW

Cross *Courting Chaos Book 1*

When a sexy drummer mistakes me for a groupie and tries to kick me out of the venue, I'm willing to chalk it up to mistaken identity. Usually everyone knows me but I shouldn't assume. Now Cross wants to make it right ini the hope that my father won't kick his band off the tour.

In trying to make amends, Cross becomes my surprise protector when I accidentally snap some pictures of his bandmate in a bad situation and he wants them deleted.

Cross being my protector has me wanting something I've never wanted before... A sexy drummer.

Growing up with a famous father has taught me many things but the number one rule has always been NEVER FALL FOR A ROCK STAR.

I guess I want to break the rules.

START READING CROSS TODAY

THE FALLOUT SERIES

A new adult romance series

Coming home is hard.
Finding out the boy you loved had a baby with your
former best friend... heartbreaking.

START READING LAST GOOD THING
TODAY

GAMBLING ON LOVE

A new adult romance series

Desperate times call for desperate measures so
Flannery Tate is selling her virginity.

START READING HIGHEST BIDDER TODAY

I you'd like to just keep up with my sales and new releases, you can follow me on BookBub!

Bookbub: https://www.bookbub.com/authors/ heather-young-nichols

Heather Young-Nichols is a USA Today Bestselling author of contemporary and paranormal romances. She writes swoony heroes and snarky heroines with a heap of romance.

When she's not writing, she's binging a show with her kids, watching baseball, or snuggling with her cuddly animals.

Find Heather on Social Media or by visiting her website.

heatheryoungnichols.com

facebook.com/heatheryoungnicholsauthor

instagram.com/heatheryoungnichols

amazon.com/Heather-Young-Nichols/e/B00KKTM54A

bookbub.com/authors/heather-young-nichols

tiktok.com/@heatheryoungnichols